Xin Publishing

Clive K. Semmens

The
Reminiscences
of
Penny Lane

Xin Publishing

Published by Xin Publishing
an imprint of Xin He Ltd.
Suite 404, 324 Regent Street
London, W1B 3HH

Story and pictures © Clive K. Semmens 2010

All rights reserved. No part of this publication can be reproduced, stored in a retrieval system, or transmitted in any form or by any means, electronic, mechanical, photocopying, recording or otherwise, without the prior permission of the publishers and/or authors.

ISBN: 978-0-9564897-4-6

Auntie Penny
by Siahir Lane

July 1977

Paul was a gentle giant – until the day he lost his rag at work, and beat up his boss. Then he went on the run. No-one knew where he was. I was distraught.

After three days he turned up, and admitted himself to the local psychiatric hospital. I visited him every day. Unsurprisingly, he didn't seem his normal self. But he was very subdued, and remorseful. After three weeks he was discharged, and came home. He didn't go back to work, but he made himself useful around the house. He still wasn't at all his old self, but he seemed to be improving day by day. I made sure he took his medication, although he seemed quite willing to do that himself, and quite capable of it.

One day about a week later, when I arrived home from work, Paul wasn't there. He'd left a note on the kitchen table saying he'd gone to visit friends, and would be back the following day. I was rather concerned, since he'd not talked about it before, and he'd not said who he was visiting, so I couldn't get in touch with him. I went to bed rather worried, and didn't get to sleep for quite a while.

I woke hearing a noise, but wasn't sure whether it was a dream, or what the noise had been. Was it the front door? I wasn't sure. I held my breath and listened intently. Yes, there were stealthy noises downstairs. Burglar? Paul?

Then I heard soft footsteps on the stairs, and the sound of the bedroom door opening. It was dark, but a little light from the city was coming in through the curtains – and there was Paul, with the big kitchen knife in his hand. He came towards me.

Instinct took over. I rolled off the bed just as Paul plunged the knife where my chest had been. As he got up off the bed, I threw the window open and leapt out onto the sloping tiles of the kitchen roof.

Luckily I was nimble in those days, and knew the walls of my garden well. I'd often climbed onto them to sit, although they were all at least six foot high and I'm only four foot eleven tall. From the kitchen roof I jumped down onto the top of the garden wall and ran along it, not looking to see if Paul was following me. I scrambled up onto the higher wall at the end, and ran along that, away from our own garden and past the ends of all the neighbours' gardens. At the end of the street was the police station, and the wall ended at the corner of the building. I clambered down onto the sloping roof of a cycle shed, and banged on an upstairs window at the back of the police station.

The window had bars on it, but I hoped at least to attract someone's attention. Eventually a policeman appeared in the yard below. He was very surprised to see a young woman in her nightclothes on the roof of the cycle shed. He fetched a ladder and I climbed down.

They found Paul wandering the streets, in a very confused state, still carrying the knife.

He was never discharged from hospital again. I continued to visit him daily, although he often didn't seem to know who I was. I think he sometimes didn't even notice I was there.

Within six months he was dead. No-one ever really knew what had happened in his head, or what he died of. They said he'd not woken up one morning, and when they'd investigated they found he was stone dead, and had apparently died in his sleep of no discernible cause. I always suspected that what actually killed him was the drugs.

Needless to say, all the while Paul was in hospital, and for quite a while thereafter, I was in a bit of a state! My prof was very understanding, and some allowances were made in the department, but I shut my mind to my private life for several hours every day, which was probably what kept me sane. I managed to keep my research going okay.

I don't think I was responsible in any way for Paul cracking up. I hope not! Maybe he always hated it when I used to thump him on the chest or on the arm. Was I guilty of domestic violence? I always thought it was playful. It was always intended that way, I don't think I ever hit him hard and certainly didn't intend to, and he never complained and never got bruises. But did it wind him up internally? I'll never know.

I've never thumped anyone since, not even playfully.

Paul never thumped me. When I tell people my boyfriend tried to stab me, they sometimes assume that he used to beat me up, but he never did. They think my wonky nose must have been caused by him, but if my wonky nose was caused by a thump, it happened in utero – and I must have given as good as I got, because my twin sister's nose is exactly the same.

Thirty-two years later I visited Burnfield again, when I was writing this book. My old street had been demolished and replaced with modern town houses, but the police station was still there, as was the pub on the opposite corner. The pub was serving meals, and I decided that would be a good place to eat.

After my meal, I sat in the pub for a while, sipping a glass of fruit juice, and people watching. As I sat there, who should come in but one of the two policemen who'd caught Paul that night. Although he looked familiar, I couldn't place who he was; but he knew who I was immediately, and came straight over to me.

"Hello, Penny! Long time no see!"

As soon as he spoke, I knew who he was. It's funny the way memory works. Apart from that one night, all the interaction we'd ever had was to say "Hi" on the street when we bumped into each other. In those days, I used to recognize him perfectly well by sight, whether he was in uniform or not.

We'd both retired by then, and we spent a couple of hours sitting there chatting. He wanted me to let him know when my book was published, and we exchanged addresses. A few weeks later I got a letter from him. He'd written an account of that night from his point of view, and with his permission I've reproduced it here as the final section of the book, before the appendices.

One thing we discussed was that since that night, both of us had started to find the sight of broken glass embedded in the tops of walls rather disturbing.

April 1978

One Saturday afternoon I was sitting on a bench in the park, brooding, when a middle-aged gent came and sat beside me. I didn't know him at all, and I'm pretty sure he'd no idea who I was, either. He said that he thought I looked depressed, and asked me whether I minded if he asked what was wrong. I'd not really looked at him until that moment. I turned to him and looked him up and down. He seemed very straightforward, it was a public place, and there were plenty of people about. I decided he was harmless.

You have to make decisions like that. You can't go through life distrusting everyone, there'd be no point in living if you did that.

I burst into tears. That's not something I do often, in fact I think it was the first time I'd done it since the day Paul first went off the rails.

Later, he said his first instinct at that moment was to put a comforting arm around me, but didn't because he thought it might frighten me. I'm not sure now whether I'd have run off immediately, or buried my face in his chest. At any rate, that's not what he did; but he put his big hand round my small one and squeezed gently. He thought I was about sixteen. I was actually twenty-nine at the time.

"You can tell me if you want to, but you don't have to say anything if you don't want to."

I looked up at him again, and tried to smile. He smiled back. I told him the whole story. He just sat there and listened. When I'd finished, he said, "What are you going to do now?"

"I don't know. I'll have to start looking for a new contract soon, my present one finishes in August."

"I know nothing about your work. I wasn't thinking of work, I was thinking of your private life. Take a break. You'll get a new contract just as easily after a six month break, I'm sure. Travel. Go to India or something like that. I've got to go now, but I expect we'll see each other around here again."

That's the best advice I've ever had, although I didn't realize it at the time. Nevertheless, I took it. What he didn't know was that I was born in India, and still had relatives there with whom I'd not been in touch since I left India when I was seven.

In the event, I got another contract at the University – which they allowed me to defer for six months. Perfect!

Both my parents were born in Evansganj, India. Three of my grandparents were born in the same area.

My mother's father was born in Ireland. He ran away from the orphanage in Cork where he'd lived for as long as he could remember, and got work on a ship; but when he found he hated it, he deserted it at the first opportunity, which turned out to be in Bombay. Exactly how much of all his many stories were true and how much fantasy, no-one was ever really sure. They certainly couldn't all have been completely true – there were too many contradictions between one story and another; but the books he said he'd stolen from a bookshop in Cork were real enough, and definitely Irish. Somehow he'd ended up in Evansganj, anyway, and married my grandmother.

Although all our earlier ancestry was English or Irish, my parents felt as though they belonged in India.

Dad got a job at the cement works. The cement works and the railway junction were the lifeblood of the town, indeed its whole reason for existing. Big brother Patrick was born a year before Indian independence, after which the family stayed on.

2nd & 3rd September 1948

My twin sister Philippa and I were born a year after independence, in the middle of the night. Dad always swore that I was born just before midnight and Pippa just after, so our birthdays are celebrated on consecutive days. He can't really have known at all because there wasn't a functional timepiece in the house, but what does it matter anyway?

Ayah said Mum and Dad couldn't really tell Pippa and me apart for the first couple of years, and which of us was Pippa and which Penny varied from day to day. Ayah could tell us apart from very early on, but she didn't dare to correct Dad. She thought Pippa was born first, and originally called Penny.

I didn't hear those stories until I met Ayah in her old age, when I went back to India in that six month break. How Pippa laughs about it now!

Until we were about eleven, we were always regarded as identical twins, and genetically we probably are. I'm not sure how Ayah knew which of us was which when we were tiny, and she couldn't tell me either. She said she just knew. A different twinkle in our eyes, or something. Apparently we went through all the early development stages together. We learnt to talk at the same time, and at first we had the same lisp. Then I started talking without a lisp. That's when Dad started to be able to tell us apart, but only for a few months, because I started copying Pippa's lisp for the devilment of it.

But from eleven onwards, I stayed pretty much the same shape and size, while Pippa didn't. I'm still four foot eleven and skinny as a rake, despite a very healthy appetite. Pippa is five foot nine and *jolly*, to use her word. She's been wearing bras ever since we were twelve; Mum got me a couple at the same time, but only because she didn't want me to be upset about it. They languish unused at the back of my undies drawer to this day, and I've still never worn one. I just don't need one.

Maybe I'd caught some infection or other, but if so my subsequent small size was its only noticeable symptom, and that wouldn't have been particularly noticeable if it wasn't for my having an identical twin. It certainly didn't affect my general health or academic progress. I went on to university and an academic career, while Pippa left school at sixteen, worked in a shop for a while, and then married a young policeman and became a housewife.

Nothing wrong with that, of course. Pippa and Gareth have got a lovely family, and truth to tell I'm a little bit jealous. I love them and their children and grandchildren to bits. Little brother Michael, born the year after we came to England, has children as well, and Big brother Patrick has grandchildren too. I don't see any of them nearly often enough.

Before I went back that first time, I only had a few disjointed memories of India. Now of course it's hard to disentangle those fragmentary memories from more recent ones.

One occasion I do remember is when a stage hypnotist came to Evansganj. Being the extrovert that I was – Pippa would never have done this – I was up on stage offering to be a subject before Mum could stop me. I'd no idea what hypnotism was all about, but he called for volunteers, and I was there before his first audience plant could make it onto the stage. He had no choice but to try to hypnotize me. Maybe I wasn't very co-operative, or maybe I'm not a very good hypnosis subject, or maybe he didn't know the first thing about real hypnosis. I remember very clearly just thinking, *What on Earth is this silly man trying to do?*

I also remember how much the audience laughed. Most of them knew me well enough, and they'd probably spotted the strangers in the audience already before they went forward.

What I don't remember about that occasion was whether everybody had paid already, or whether the poor fellow was relying on a collection. Most itinerant stage acts in India do rely on collections rather than an entrance fee, so he probably didn't do very well in Evansganj. (The reason they do this is the disparity of wealth in India: an entrance fee is either too small to make much money out of the wealthier members of the audience, or too big to attract a respectable number to the show.)

I still tend to think of *The Emperor's New Clothes* whenever anyone mentions hypnosis.

January 1956

The first period I remember really well was the trip coming from India to England the first time – nearly three weeks in a big steamship. We three kids all loved it, but I think I had the best time of all. I'd developed an interest in how things worked, and the ship's chief engineer had noticed that and taken a shine to me. How the world has changed! Imagine today's parents allowing a seven year old girl to spend most of her time alone with the ship's engineer, down in the engine room or happily splashing around in the oily water below the bottom deck looking at bilge pumps and helping to clear their intakes! But I came to no harm and learnt a great deal.

Arriving in London in February was quite a shock, for our parents as much as for us kids I think. It was really cold. We were used to it being cold, occasionally even frosty, early on a winter's morning in Evansganj, but snow was new to us, and the idea that it could stay cold all day was new too. But at least it was warm in the tenement in Whitechapel that we moved into.

Dad got a job as a bus driver. He said it was a bit of a comedown after being a shift foreman in Evansganj, but it was a lot better paid. Against that, the cost of living was a lot higher too. Overall he reckoned we were quite a lot better off, but whether he really believed that I don't know. Maybe he just couldn't come to terms with having made such a big mistake, if such it was. Dad drove buses from then until the day he retired, and seemed happy enough.

I remember being absolutely spellbound by the gas water heater over the kitchen sink. It was an Ascot – I can see its name written on it in my mind's eye right now. For some reason it had a spherical end on the cranked pipe that delivered the water. I remember that very clearly, and have to this day not worked out why it had that spherical end. There was a similar device over the big cast iron bath in the bathroom, but it didn't work. We had to carry hot water from the kitchen in a couple of big enamelled iron jugs, back and forth several times.

There were gas fires too. Dad didn't like them. He said coal was much cheaper, but Mum liked them because they were cleaner and less trouble.

March 1962

Big brother Patrick had started studying Chemistry at school, and I was fascinated. I was interested in Space Travel, and rockets – and here was how to make rockets! Well, I couldn't get normal rocket fuels, but reading Patrick's chemistry textbook I could see that there would be lots of alternative combinations of things that would do. I could get hold of something that would be a good second best.

Patrick's book wasn't enough. I scoured the public library. I found a couple of secondhand bookshops on Charing Cross Road, and pored over old books there, too. I didn't buy any, but the proprietors were kindly old men who seemed inclined to indulge a polite little girl – I was thirteen, but looked about eleven – who came alone to find and take notes from undergraduate level textbooks.

Fuel was no problem. Sugar would do very nicely. I needed an oxidizing agent.

In those days, you could buy pure sodium chlorate as a weedkiller. (These days it's always mixed with a fire retardant.) The ironmongers in Mile End Road knew me. I was the little girl who bought all kinds of odd things in very small quantities. I don't think he'd have sold sodium chlorate in quantity to just any child, and he did impress upon me the need to "be careful", and questioned whether I really did want so much. But he sold it to me. Three times in total.

Incidentally, the chemist knew me too. This isn't connected with the rocketry story, but now seems a good moment to mention that I bought half a kilogram of sodium metal in the chemists on Mile End Road at about the same time, for a different project. I didn't really want as much as half a kilogram, but that was the minimum quantity he could get from his suppliers. It came as chunks an inch square by about an inch and a half long, in paraffin oil in a plastic jar. It was a special order, not the kind of thing a high street pharmacist normally stocks!

I don't think even an adult would be able to buy sodium quite so easily nowadays. The anti-terrorist squad would be down on you like a ton of bricks for just asking about it .

It cost me eight shillings and threepence, an absolute fortune in those days. Four week's pocket money and a bit – mine and Pippa's, bless her.

Back to rocketry!

Dad had a shed on the allotments, not far from our tenement. He'd made a nice, solid workbench out of timber he'd salvaged from a bomb site – old joists, I think. He'd picked up an old metalworking vice from an army surplus shop in Aldgate, and mounted that on the bench.

This was the ideal place for my experiments. Dad knew I did all kinds of things in his shed, and generally didn't inquire too deeply into exactly what I was doing.

I had plans to make two rockets. One was to fire upwards, just to see how well it performed; the other was to attach to my bicycle, to see what it was like riding a rocket-propelled bicycle.

I wanted to bench test one of my rockets before actually firing one. I'd even managed to rig up a test device to measure the thrust. The test device was mounted in Dad's vice, and the exhaust from the rocket was supposed to go out of the open door.

I made the rockets in some thick cardboard tubing I scavenged from the rubbish at one of the local businesses. The first one was about two and a half inches in diameter and fifteen inches long.

I was a bit worried about being close to it when I ignited it, so I did it remotely with a battery and a bit of resistance wire. I'm glad I did.

Dad's beautiful bench with the vice on the end just stood there unperturbed. Bits of the shed were scattered all over the allotments.

Dad was amazingly good about it. He spent his days off over the next few weeks building a new, bigger and stronger shed. He didn't ban me from using the new shed, not for a single day. He asked me please to be careful, and complimented me on my wisdom in not having been too close!

He didn't tell a soul outside the family. Anyone who asked was told that he'd "had a bit of an accident". He swore Mum and Patrick and Pippa to secrecy. Little Michael didn't know until years later what had happened.

That's the kind of Dad you need.

Maybe I wasn't the kind of daughter Dad needed though, but if that's the case he never let it show.

Just two months later I bench tested my second attempt, and fortunately that went smoothly. The rocket fired for twelve seconds, and the peak thrust was fifty-five pounds. My thrust meter only recorded the peak. I'd no means of knowing whether the thrust was reasonably steady, or just a brief peak and much weaker before and after it.

I was ready to fire a rocket. Upwards. Where would the burnt out bit of cardboard tube and the stick end up? I'd not even thought about that, but the stick was heavy enough to do someone an injury if they were unlucky enough to be in the way of its descent.

I've still no idea where it landed. I don't know how high it went, but it was pretty high. I'm not sure whether I lost sight of it because it stopped firing, or because it was simply too high to see the tiny bright speck against a blue sky.

While I'm thinking about allotments, here's a little observation for the pot. A lot of people think it's a modern middle-class affectation to be growing fancy vegetables on the allotments, and that the old working-class allotment holders only grew potatoes and carrots and parsnips and onions and beetroot and peas and beans and cabbages and sprouts and cauliflowers and tomatoes and marrows and pumpkins and cucumbers and raspberries and strawberries and currants and gooseberries.

Don't you believe it. Those Whitechapel allotments were a hundred percent working class. There wasn't a toff in sight. Toffs didn't do allotments in those days. Sure, there were all those regular vegetables and fruit. But there were aubergines and courgettes and garlic and capsicums and artichokes (both sorts) and chillies...and things the toffs still haven't heard of, like scorzonera and cardoon and...

And it wasn't just my Dad. It was lots of the chaps, and yes, a few ladies too. They were growing all sorts long before Dad arrived – it wasn't that he brought fancy ideas from India or anything.

I do not recommend the rocket propelled bicycle. I tried that twice.

The first time, the bicycle shot out from under me, and the exhaust from the rocket gave me a burn on my bare right shin whose scar I still bear to this day. I landed hard on my backside on the road. My bicycle skidded down the road on its side, and ended up spinning round and round like a horizontal Catherine wheel. One pedal lost its end cap, but otherwise the bike was, remarkably, pretty much unscathed.

I kept my burn secret for three weeks, from everyone except Pippa. Whether anyone else wondered why I took to wearing jeans all the time, I don't know. Jeans aren't the most comfortable thing to wear over an amateurish dressing on a bad burn, but they do hide it nicely.

Nothing daunted, three weeks later I tried again. I made sure that this time I was well attached to the bicycle, with a strap round my back attached to the handlebars. The rocket was mounted rather higher than before, behind the saddle rather than alongside the chain. I did indeed stay aboard.

It's not easy to control an ordinary pushbike at that speed, though. Maybe it's not possible at all. Certainly I didn't manage it.

The initial acceleration was terrific. I was ecstatic. It worked!

But steering gets jolly hard, and then begins wobble rapidly from side to side, before the front wheel finally swings uncontrollably right over to one side and you fall off.

That much I remember very clearly. It can only have taken a couple of seconds, but the whole sequence of events is indelibly imprinted in my memory. But if you're still strapped to the bike, and the rocket's still pushing the bike, that's not the end of it.

I really don't remember what happened after I hit the road. Witnesses said I skidded down the road on my side for quite a distance, and then spun round and round in the middle of the road for a bit.

My bike didn't survive the excitement this time. Luckily I did, without even a single broken bone. But I lost an awful lot of skin, and completely wrecked all my clothes.

Mum wasn't quite as forgiving as Dad had been, and told Dad off in no uncertain terms "for encouraging her", which I never thought was fair at all. He'd never really encouraged me, unless not discouraging me amounted to encouraging me.

I was NOT called Penny Lane after the Beatles song. I was called Penny Lane *before* the Beatles song. Oh, how I hated that song. It was popular just when I was doing my A levels, and wherever I went lots of the boys whistled it.

My full name is actually Penelope Louise Joyce Lane. My parents, in small town India, had never heard of PLJ, so they can't be blamed for my nicknames. As soon as I started school in England, I was Pure Lemon Juice, which mutated to Sourpuss as we got older.

In the British community in Evansganj – well, the poor British community, anyway, I don't know about the toffs – a popular way of forming a pet name for a child was to run the first and middle names, or short forms of them, together. So Philippa Elizabeth Ann was Pippa-Liz, and I was Penny-Lou. Nice, affectionate names. There weren't any penny-in-the-slot public toilets in Evansganj, nobody had ever heard of such a thing. The smallest coin in India in those days was one pice, so they'd have been pice-in-the-slot anyway, if they'd existed. Whether Patrick had cottoned on more quickly to the English meaning of my Evansganj pet name than the rest of the family, I don't know, but I do know that it was he who told children at school. So then I was

Penny-Loo as well, but the teachers decided to call a halt to that. It went underground for a while, and finally disappeared.

During my undergraduate years, my best friends were William Ackroyd and Benjamin Bernstein. Bill and Ben. With my size and shape it was inevitable that I became Little Weed. Ho hum. I didn't mind though, it was always used affectionately.

We three were members of the University Rock Climbing Club. Although my reach wasn't as long as anyone else's, I was light and supple and very wiry which more than made up for it in most situations. I gained the respect of a lot of pretty tough blokes. There were a few girls in the club, but Little Weed was the only one who could climb with the best of the blokes.

In our second year, the three of us joined the Potholing Club as well, and there I was at a huge advantage.

I enjoyed those years. Nearly every weekend rock climbing or potholing meant I had to work extra hard during the week to keep up with my studies, but I managed. It probably taught me the discipline that I'd never really needed at school, and probably thereby actually helped my academic work.

I've remained friends with Bill and Ben ever since.

They started an engineering company together several years after we'd all finished our PhDs. Believing my maths to be better than theirs, they asked me if I was interested in joining them. At first, they didn't really have enough of my kind of work to keep me busy anywhere near full-time, so I acted as a part-time consultant and continued teaching in school, which I'd taken up after a few years doing research.

May 1992

One of the jobs I did for them involved several visits to one of their clients, Pericor Engineering, and on the fourth visit I was called in to see the personnel manager, Bob. He said, "You're only working with Ackroyd and Bernstein part time, aren't you? How would you like to come and work full-time for us?"

I said I couldn't do that without consulting Bill and Ben first, and that I'd probably want to continue working part-time for them. Bob pointed to the phone, and then said, "or would you prefer to talk to them privately?"

I wasn't sure about leaving teaching anyway, which I really enjoyed and felt fulfilled in, but the money was too tempting. I rang Bill from home that evening, and the following day I accepted Bob's offer. I was free to take unpaid leave to work with Bill and Ben whenever they needed me. It seemed perfect.

It turned out that it wasn't perfect at all, but the money was a lot better than teaching, there's no denying that.

JUNE 1994

"We'd like you to do a special project for us. It's probably quite a challenge, but we know you like a challenge."

"Fire away. I'm all ears."

"It's really mainly for Bob. You explain it, Bob."

"You know how Pericor keeps everything on file, for legal reasons. Every version of every file created in the company, every file downloaded from elsewhere, every email sent or received, every website visited?"

"I didn't actually know that, but you don't surprise me. I can see how some of that information could be very useful in various legal battles. There's an obvious problem with it, of course: it's an awful lot of stuff to trawl through for the crucial nugget of information that you need. I imagine that it's all pretty much unstructured. It's hard to see how you would structure such a database, or at least, how you'd structure it in any very helpful way."

"That's right, and that's where your project comes in. What we want is a program to do the trawling for us, a program that we can give a question to, that then goes off and searches all the records for everything relevant it can find."

Since Bob was the personnel manager, I wondered why this was his project. Well, not really. I had by then learnt a little bit about company politics. But I didn't say anything about that.

"A general one? That's a very tall order. It'd be hard enough trawling for answers to specific, predetermined questions that the programmer knows the meaning of. A program to analyse a question written in plain English by someone who doesn't know what the program can and can't understand, is a problem of a different order. I don't see how I can expect the user to learn a special formal language to write the query in, but without that, I don't see this as a feasible project for me. Not even if you let me have a small team."

"You're making more of this than you need to. We can give you a list of specific questions up front."

"That means I'd have to be trusted with prior information about legal issues. That's a pretty big responsibility."

What I was being asked to do is available off-the-peg today of course. Much more than what I was being asked to do, in fact. But it wasn't in 1995.

"Aren't you ready for that level of responsibility? Perhaps we'll have to find someone else to do the project."

"I didn't say I wasn't. All I was wondering was whether you were ready to give me that level of responsibility."

"If we can't find someone to write a program that can analyse a query written in plain English – and we'd already considered that, and realized it was going to be very hard – we've got to give someone that responsibility. Jim said he thought you were probably the girl for the job."

Girl. I was forty-five. But I didn't say anything about that either. People tended to forget. I didn't look it.

"I'm flattered. There's another issue of responsibility. I need to know what the data's like. As I said, I imagine it's pretty much unstructured. That is, its structure – everything's got one, really – is presumably unplanned and a bit random. The only way I can get a handle on the way it's organized is to actually look at it, which means I'll be seeing a lot of confidential stuff. That's an even bigger responsibility than knowing what your questions are. Probably."

"Yes. We were aware of that, too, but we know you're a trustworthy member of the team."

"There's another little niggly thing. You said, 'every website visited'. Are the actual contents viewed kept on record, or just the URLs? If you only keep URLs, they may not connect to anything any more, or they may connect to something that's different from what they connected to when they were originally visited."

"We keep copies of what was actually downloaded to the users' computers. And the URLs."

"Okay. So... give me a list of your specific questions, and access to the database, and I'll see what I can come up with. Actually, I could do better than that. Give me a short list of typical questions, nothing that is actually a legal issue at the moment or in the foreseeable future, and I'll think about how I can restructure the database to make it easier to answer questions of that general kind. That is, restructure what we've got now, and redesign the way the data is gathered so that it drops straight into my new structure."

"Now you're giving us a tall order. How about one question at a time?"

"Well, that doesn't give me much to go on, to decide how best to restructure the data. But it sounds as though you have a specific query you want answered right now. In itself, that's a much easier problem; but it doesn't help much with preparing for future queries."

"Don't worry too much about future queries. We'll cross those bridges when we come to them."

"Okay, so what's your specific query?"

Bob explained it.

"So what you're saying is that you want me to write a program that trawls through all the records, all the emails, everything else it can find, relates it to each employee, and compiles a database of people's foibles – that you can use against them when you want to get rid of them?"

When you want to get rid of them for some other reason that you'd rather not make public – but I thought I'd leave that unsaid, too.

"I wouldn't have put it quite that way, but in a nutshell, yes, that's pretty much it."

"I'm sorry to say that I've got a pretty serious foible myself. I've got scruples. What's worse, I've got an infectious form of the disease. I think you're probably going to have to fire me."

And I'll see you in court if you do, I thought. I wished I'd had a voice recording of the meeting.

I'm not sure about the morality of taking voice recordings of meetings covertly. I don't think they'd have had any scruples about doing it themselves, if they'd had any reason to want to, but that'd be no excuse for me to have done it. Does the very fact that it was a meeting between figures in authority and a subordinate give the subordinate an automatic moral right to record proceedings covertly? I'd certainly defend someone else's right to do it. But I'm not sure I'd claim that right myself.

They got Geoff to do the deed. They never got a chance to fire me, because I resigned first. I'd started looking for a new job with a different company straight away, and was lucky enough to get a job with Ladoca Ltd. pretty quickly, before Geoff had even finished the project.

I'd have loved to have sued Pericor for constructive dismissal, but it would have been a difficult case to prove without getting Geoff to give evidence. I know he didn't like Pericor much, but I don't think he'd have been prepared to take the risk of giving evidence against them. I couldn't have brought myself to ask him anyway.

And it probably wouldn't have been a good career move for me, either. Not really. Bill and Ben still didn't really have enough of my kind of work to keep me busy full-time.

It wasn't long before they did though, and I only worked at Ladoca for three years before leaving to move up to Edinburgh to join them. I worked with them until I retired last year.

At the time of my first trip back to India, my oldest nieces and nephews were still small children. I lived a long way from everyone else in the family, but I saw them from time to time and knew them all quite well.

I didn't really know my relatives in India at all. None of us had seen any of them since we left. I knew a little bit about them because Mum sometimes got short notes with Christmas cards from Grandma and Uncle John. Mum always sent a letter with a card at Christmas.

Both grandads and the other grandma had died within a few years of our leaving India, and Dad had completely lost touch with both his brothers. They were much older than him, and had left Evansganj to go and work in Bombay when he was still small.

I wrote to Uncle John to tell him I was coming, but never received a reply. I was confident of simply finding somewhere to stay whether I managed to find the family or not, and fully intended to travel around India independently quite a bit in my six months anyway. But I thought I'd go to Evansganj first.

OCTOBER 1978

India was quite a shock, even though I'd spent the first seven years of my life there, and knew quite a lot about it in theory. I stayed in a guesthouse in Delhi for a couple of days, and then caught the train to Evansganj.

The train had already done a couple of hundred miles before arriving in Delhi, and was two hours late and very crowded. I'd reserved a berth, but until nine in the evening anyone can sit anywhere. Your berth is exclusively yours only from nine until six – or, to be strictly accurate, from the place where the train should have reached by nine in the evening, until the place it should reach by six. It was midnight before I got my bed to myself.

But I didn't care, everyone was so friendly, and all of them wanted to practice their English on me and feed me. I've heard tales of travellers being given drugged food or drinks on trains, but these things don't happen often, and I'm sure that they happen even less often on trains that rarely have foreign tourists on them. And there were plenty of other people around, so I felt pretty safe.

It's a twenty-one hour journey according to the timetable, and we were five hours late by the time we arrived in Evansganj. It was beginning to get dark by then. I had Uncle John's address, of course, and I got a rickshaw to take me.

A young man about my own age answered the door.

"Does John O'Malley live here? Is he at home?" I didn't try to use my rusty, childish Hindi on him. I hoped he'd understand English.

He turned and shouted into the house, "Dad!" just like that, in English.

Uncle John appeared. He looked older of course, but he was the same Uncle John I remembered from twenty-two years earlier. He took one look at me and grabbed me in a big bear hug, lifting me clean off my

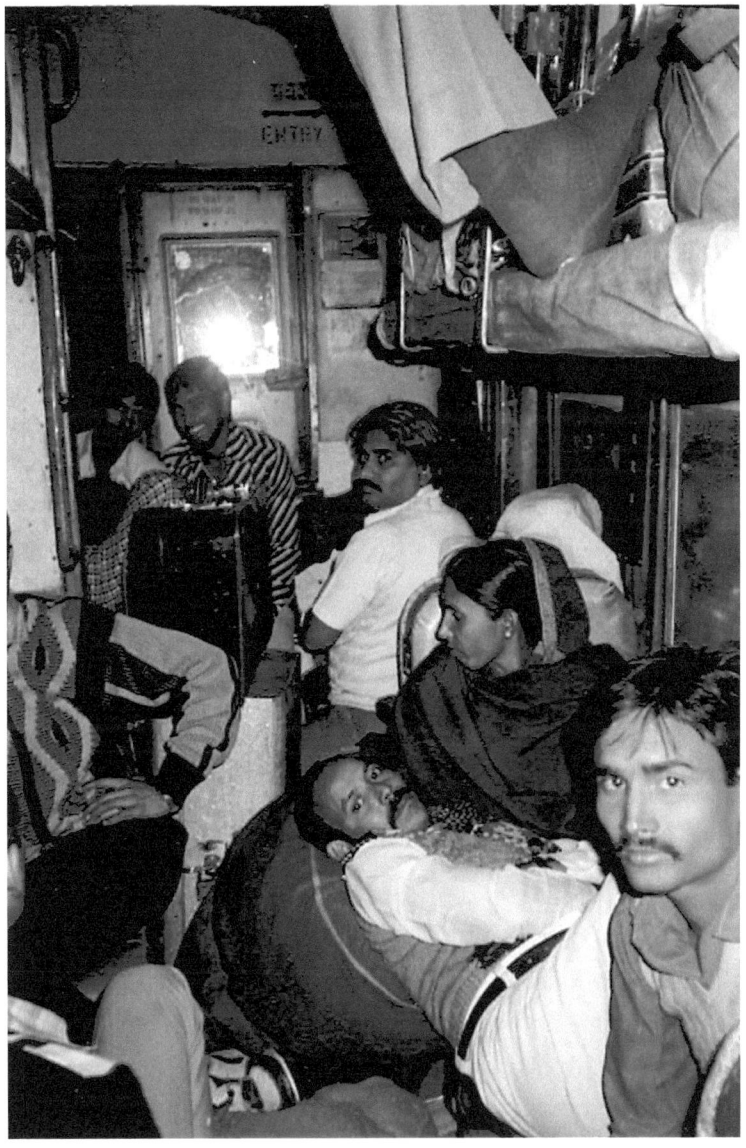

feet. Then he put me down and held me at arm's length and looked me up and down.

"Well!" he said at last, "Is it Penny-Lou or Pippa-Liz? How am I supposed to know? We never thought we'd see you again!"

"Ravi – go and get your Mum, and tell Shanti to make some chai."

The young man disappeared into the house. "He's your son? He seems about my age!"

"Yes, he's my son – your cousin. He is your age, near enough. Just a year younger than you. Come inside and sit down. We've got an awful lot to talk about!"

A very black lady with silver hair, a very round face and a beaming smile appeared. She was even smaller than me.

"Chhoti, this is – ah – this is your niece, but I still don't know whether it's Penny-Lou or Pippa-Liz."

"I'm Penny. Pippa's much bigger than me."

A surprised look appeared on Uncle John's face, but he went on, "Penny-Lou, this is Chhoti, my wife. That was Ravi, our eldest, you just met. Now let's go inside and sit down."

Chhoti is Hindi for Little (feminine), or Little One, and is often used as a nickname for little girls, but I'd never heard it as an adult's name before.

The house brought back memories of the one Grandma and Grandad lived in when I was little, which was very similar. The furniture looked as though it might have been the same pieces – all obviously handmade from local timber, aged to a lovely dark chocolate brown, and a little irregular here and there. The three of us sat at a small table. A girl of about twenty brought a tray with three cups of chai and a glass of water. Ravi followed her in and sat down. The girl put the tray on the table and went and stood in the corner of the room looking at me shyly.

"Shanti, Shanti – no need to be shy. Penny-Lou, this is your cousin Shanti. Shanti, this is your cousin Penny-Lou."

Well, I knew from Mum that Uncle John was married and had three children. Their ages were a bit of a puzzle, but I was beginning to guess.

"Yes, you've guessed, I can see. I wonder what your mother will say?"

"She doesn't know? I was beginning to wonder whether she'd been keeping secrets from me. If you'd rather I didn't tell her, that's easy enough. She wouldn't think anything of the facts themselves, but she'd be hurt that you'd never told her."

"She wouldn't think anything of the facts themselves? She's changed a lot in twenty years, then."

"There's been a lot of water under a lot of bridges in that time. I lived with a chap I wasn't married to for three years. She came to terms with that in the end."

We talked and talked. Ravi put in the odd word from time to time, but Chhoti and Shanti said not a word. They just sat and stood there smiling, and sometimes laughing with the rest of us. It was nearly all Uncle John and me.

After a while, Chhoti and Shanti slipped quietly out of the room. A little later Shanti popped her head round the door and whispered to Ravi, "Idhar ao!" – Hindi for "Come here." Ravi excused himself and slipped out too. He was gone for about half an hour, but then he was back with us.

Shanti brought another round of chai and some sweetmeats, then disappeared again.

I told John all about Paul, and my University work, and Patrick's and Pippa's families. I learnt how he'd lived a double life for years, with no-one in Evansganj knowing about Chhoti and their children in Dhumshakti, ten miles up the line where he worked at the railway station. Well, no-one who didn't keep diplomatically silent, anyway! Then, when Grandad died, how they'd decided to get married and make it all official, mainly so that Ravi could move to the mission school in Evansganj, that was so much better than the government school in Dhumshakti.

I could imagine how it was all quite a scandal in a rather puritanical white protestant Christian community in a small town in India. I gathered that attitudes had changed a lot in Evansganj – and suspected that John and Chhoti had had a lot to do with the changes. Well done John and Chhoti! But that was all eighteen years ago, and apart from John and Grandma, all the other white people in Evansganj had either died or left since then.

Kamal, their other son, between Ravi and Shanti, was working in Dhumshakti, and only came home two nights a week – different nights depending on his rota. John joked about him maybe having a family there and no-one knowing about it, but he thought it a bit unlikely. "I think he knows it wouldn't be necessary to keep it secret! And it would be hard anyway, with so many of Chhoti's relatives there."

Chhoti and Shanti appeared with a massive feast and set it on the table in front of the three of us, then disappeared into the shadows. John called them back to the table, "Penny-Lou is family, not an outsider! Come and eat with us." Beaming smiles and a little reluctance, but John insisted, and they did eat with us – but still they didn't say a word.

The meal was wonderful. Ravi had been sent out to procure a chicken from a neighbour who kept them, and had killed it on the way home so I wouldn't hear anything – but I only learnt that later.

After the meal, we carried on talking deep into the night. Chhoti and Shanti went to bed, but then got up again when John wanted to make arrangements for where I was going to sleep. I was to sleep in Shanti's bed, and Shanti would sleep with some blankets on the kitchen floor. I said no, I'd sleep on the floor – I was used to sleeping anywhere. "I'm used to sleeping on the kitchen floor!" Shanti insisted; but I wasn't having it. Eventually I saw the bed – it was wide, nearly as wide as a typical English double bed, and Shanti and I ended up sleeping side by side.

When the two of us were alone, Shanti broke her silence, and we talked and talked and talked. Shanti kept switching back and forth between English and Hindi when she got excitable, which brought my Hindi flooding back, and we ended up chatting in a complete muddle of Hindi and English. We laughed and laughed. It was dawn before we finally went to sleep – or I did, anyway. I think Shanti got up when I went to sleep, but I'm not sure, it could have been a bit later. She'd certainly been up and about for a long time by the time I surfaced not long before midday.

John and Ravi had already gone to work when I got up. John worked at the goods yard, and Ravi worked at the cement works. Chhoti and Shanti both worked in the mission hospital in Evansganj, but they were both on their day off. They took me round to Grandma's house as soon as we'd eaten – lunch for them, breakfast for me, but the same meal anyway.

Grandma was still living in the same house that she and Grandpa had lived in twenty odd years before – for much longer than that, in fact. Both Mum and John had been born and raised there.

Grandma was still sprightly, and said she'd had a feeling she'd see at least one of us before she died. She complained that Mum hadn't sent her a card last Christmas, and I said that she always did, every year. Then Grandma got to complaining about the Indian postal service instead.

There was a knock at the door. "That'll be Miriam," said Grandma. "You answer it, Penny-Lou. She'll be so pleased!"

Miriam was our Ayah when we were children. I'd always known her name was Miriam, but no-one had ever used her name talking to me before – she was always Ayah.

"Penny-Lou!" Uncle John hadn't known whether I was Penny or Pippa – but Ayah did.

I didn't remember Ayah as small at all. In reality, she was even smaller than Chhoti.

Hugging isn't the usual thing amongst Indians, but this was my Ayah, who'd cuddled Pippa and me every day for the first seven years of our lives. It was my turn to hug my tiny Ayah. There were tears in her eyes, the first I'd seen in India.

It wasn't until many years later, after Ayah died, that I learnt something about her history.

She had been a member of the Christian congregation in one of the outlying villages. Like many Indian Christians, she hadn't married young like most of her Hindu peers. In her late twenties – probably, no-one knew exactly which year she'd been born – she'd married a much older man.

For several years, they had remained sadly childless. In those days, in that culture, if a couple remained childless it was quite normal for a man to blame his wife and abandon her. But Ayah's husband was a better man than that, and remained faithful to her. Then, probably in her late thirties, she fell pregnant. She was heavily pregnant with their first child when her husband died.

It was a difficult birth, and there wasn't much help available in the village. An older woman, experienced in helping at childbirth but not trained, did the best she could, but it was clear than neither Ayah nor the baby were well. A boy was sent by bicycle to the mission compound in a village fifteen miles away, and the missionary – not a qualified doctor, but experienced in such matters because he'd found it necessary to be – came and patched Ayah up as best he could. Ayah and the baby were despatched to the mission hospital in Evansganj, but it was a long and difficult journey in those days. It still is a long and difficult journey, but it was much worse in 1948. The baby was dead by the time they reached Evansganj.

Ayah survived, but the doctor in Evansganj said she'd never be able to have another child.

She had no hope of getting married again, and once she'd recovered sufficiently to get out and about, she went looking for work – just at the time the doctor told my parents that he thought Mum was going to have twins. He was right. That was Pippa and me.

Having once made contact, I did my best to keep in touch. I exchanged letters with Shanti and Uncle John at intervals, but the postal service in and out of Evansganj is not the most reliable. I'm not sure exactly where the problems are – whether they're in Evansganj itself, or somewhere on the way. I gave up trying to send photographs. Nothing thicker than an envelope with a single folded sheet of paper seemed to have any chance at all of arriving.

OCTOBER 1981

Happily I did get the letter inviting me to Shanti's wedding. Ravi had been all the way to Kanpur to post it, just to be sure. Flights to India around Christmas time are particularly expensive, and it was quite a stretch for my budget, but I just had to go. They told me later that inviting me was simply their way of telling me about the wedding, without offending me by saying I wasn't invited. They didn't actually expect me to come, but were very pleased when I wrote and said I was coming. I sent two letters, on different days and one in an aerogram and the other in an envelope to make sure they got at least one, and both of them arrived.

Their reply never reached me despite being posted in Kanpur, so I didn't know I was going to three weddings in two weeks until I arrived. Both Ravi and Kamal had decided, with their fiancees, to change their plans so the weddings would all be while I was in Evansganj.

July 1975

I'd bought the house Paul and I had been living in very cheap, because it was scheduled for demolition at some unspecified time in the future. I'd almost got the purchase price in my savings, and Dad gave me the rest. He'd already helped Patrick with the deposit for his house, and had lent me a lot of money when I was doing my PhD, which he'd refused to let me pay back – all out of his savings from working as a bus driver. Our Dad really was someone special.

April 1979

Shortly after I got back from India, I got the letter informing me that the house was due to be compulsorily purchased for demolition. I got back almost as much as I'd paid for it, which wasn't bad considering I'd lived in it for nearly four years. If I'd got nothing back it wouldn't have been terribly expensive considered as rent.

But it did mean I needed to find somewhere to live, and the whole of the compulsory purchase price, plus my savings, didn't amount to a deposit on a decent house. I'm sure Dad would have found the money, but I was beginning to feel it was unfair to ask – I was thirty, not twenty-three! So I went looking for somewhere to rent.

I was very lucky. I really landed on my feet. I asked around at the department. Sheila, the prof's secretary, said that her nephew Neil had a lovely flat in a former vicarage a couple of miles from the centre of town, and that one of the other three flats was about to come vacant. She put me in touch with her nephew, and we met up over a coffee in town. I think Sheila might have been trying her hand at matchmaking, but as I discovered after I moved into the flat, Neil had a girlfriend that his family didn't know about yet. But whatever the truth of that might have been, the flat was lovely, I was the first person to enquire about it, the landlords seemed to approve of me, and I lived there for fifteen years.

An important part of what makes a rented property nice or nasty is the landlord. Generally, I'm sure that the more remote the landlord, the better. Mr and Mrs Oldfield lived in a bungalow built in the grounds of the big house, but that was absolutely fine, because they were absolutely lovely. You couldn't ask for better landlords.

One of their idiosyncrasies was that they never raised anybody's rent. Each time a new tenant moved in, they set the rent at the current market rate, but that's what it remained as long as you stayed.

C̲h̲r̲i̲s̲t̲m̲a̲s̲ 1981, I̲n̲d̲i̲a̲

I felt like an old hand on my second trip to India. I didn't even bother with a guest house in Delhi. I got off the plane, caught the bus into town, went to a bank and changed some money, and then went straight to the station. The next train all the way to Evansganj wasn't for another fourteen hours and there were no berths available on it, so I got a fast day train to Kanpur. I knew that in Kanpur I'd have to get the same train I'd have caught anyway, but I hoped there'd be some berths from Kanpur. Add to that, I'd get to spend some time in Kanpur, which I didn't know at all, rather than Delhi, where I'd spent some time before.

Christmas is a busy time on Indian trains – well, every day is a busy time on Indian trains, but Christmas especially so. The Kanpur quota was all taken, too. So I was going to have to travel in an unreserved carriage ("bogie" in Indian English). Ho hum.

I spent the night in a station rest room. In the morning, I got breakfast in the station restaurant – omelette on toast, with chutney and chai – and then went and waited on the platform for my train.

I managed to find a place on a wooden bench. I took off my sandals, leaving them on the platform underneath the bench, and tucked my feet under me on the bench.

I'd been there a while, when a young fellow with a box of shoe polishing materials – a *polish wallah* – came along the platform. I saw him polishing several men's shoes for them, and receiving a small sum from each, although more men declined his services.

Then he spotted me, and my dusty, scuffed sandals under the bench. I saw his face light up. *A white lady! Money!*

"Sandal polish, lady?" In English.

I resisted the temptation to reply in Hindi. "How much?"

"Five rupees."

Well, I knew the normal price was more like one rupee, but I also understood that I was a rare opportunity for him to make a little more, and it's only fair that the poor in a poor country make a little extra from relatively wealthy people from wealthy countries. But equally, I didn't want to spoil him. This time I replied in Hindi, much to his surprise.

"I'll give you two-fifty."

"Okay."

He did a beautiful job. I handed him a five rupee note. He fumbled in his box for some change, but I told him, "No, keep the change. It's a present."

He turned his face away, but not quickly enough to avoid me seeing his wide smile. He knew I knew it was too much, so he wasn't ripping me off – he knew it really was a present, which I'm certain was more satisfactory for him just as it was for me.

I say " it's only fair that the poor in a poor country make a little extra from relatively wealthy people from wealthy countries" but really that's a gross understatement – it's a minuscule improvement in a very unfair situation. But it's a very unfair situation that no-one can correct single-handed. And if that sounds like an excuse for meanness, it's a hard accusation to rebuff.

But what would the consequences be if one shared one's good fortune equally with everyone one met? If everyone did it as a matter of routine, it would very rapidly result in the elimination of unfairness – but of course they don't, and the actual result would be one more person in extreme poverty, and a small increase in the number of moderately wealthy people. And that's assuming that there weren't any more complex effects – which would very likely include violence. Ho hum.

That said, it's not a conundrum I've really disentangled to my own satisfaction. I've seen other people's suggested solutions, that some of them seem satisfied with, but none of them satisfy me.

With the help of a coolie, I crammed myself into an unreserved bogie. I don't know how many people there were in there, but it must have been at least three hundred.

I sat on a long bench seat with my feet on the bench in front of me, and my knees under my chin. I couldn't put my feet on the floor, because there was an old lady sitting there in much the same posture. The floor was covered with people and boxes and people on boxes. There were more people sitting on the berth above us. I was very glad I was wearing salwar kameej, but other women were quite cheerfully sitting in similar postures in sarees.

Young women wearing salwar kameej.

The coolie had come into the compartment with me. He made people make room on the seat for me. There was a netting parcel rack above the seats the other side of the corridor, and he shuffled people's parcels on it to make room for my rucksack. I gave him five rupees, and thanked him in Hindi. After he'd gone, everyone told me I was too generous and should learn the value of money, and they wanted to know how I knew Hindi.

Some people seemed to manage to sleep like that, I don't know how. I dozed fitfully a few times. Every time we stopped, someone seemed to be getting out, and more people came cramming in. I knew we were due to arrive in Evansganj at about one in the afternoon, and from mid-day onwards I was watching out of the window for Rojasganj (pronounced Rogers Gunge, and probably named after some Angrezi called Rogers), the station before Evansganj, so I could retrieve my rucksack and make my way to the door and be ready to get off. It was getting dark by the time we arrived.

I've travelled unreserved a few times since then, but never at quite such a busy time. It's never been quite so crowded. And I've learnt other tricks of Indian travel, but of that more some other time.

That was a fantastic holiday. Having decided not to hang around in Delhi, I arrived in Evansganj a couple of days earlier than I was expected, which was lucky, otherwise I'd have had no time to gather my wits after the journey.

Ravi and Sushila were getting married just four days after I arrived. Sushila worked at the mission hospital with Shanti and Chhoti, but she came from Bartola, a village out in the wilds, forty-five miles south of Dhumshakti. Getting to Bartola was quite a journey, that took all of a long day.

Although I'd spent six months in India three years earlier, I'd never done a journey like that one. The train to Dhumshakti I was familiar with, but the bus out to Bartola was something else. I thought trains could be impossibly crowded, but they're spacious luxury compared to the country buses. I've ridden in those country buses quite a lot over the years, and they're nearly always fantastically crowded – but I've never since been in one quite as crowded as that first one was. That's what happens when there's a wedding party of fifty odd people added to the typical load, of course.

For the first ten miles or so, the road was well surfaced, and the ride smooth enough except for a couple of times when we met a truck coming the other way and had to go half off the road to get past it. But at Dhuma our route left the main road, and for the last thirty miles the road was just a rough track, and we averaged less than eight miles an hour.

The bus looked as if it was about to fall to bits, but it must have been as tough as old boots – an English bus really would have fallen to bits if it had tried to do the trip. It would have been a difficult road in a

Land Rover. (I know about driving Land Rovers on the rough, I've done a lot of it.)

The bouncing and shaking and jolting was incredible. I'd never experienced anything like it. I was treated like royalty, though – well, relatively. I wasn't sitting on anyone's knee, and no-one was sitting on mine. I offered to have a little boy on my knee, and his mother was grateful, but the little boy wouldn't come to me. So he sat on her knee, while she sat half on one old lady's knee, and half on another's.

There were six people in that particular seat, designed for three, and the same size as a seat for two in an English bus. Five of the six were adults.

The aisle was full of standing passengers, and I mean full. They were pressed together like sardines. Yet somehow the conductor managed to worm his way through and collect everybody's fare.

What it was like for the people on the roof, literally dozens of them, I dread to think. Apart from all the people, there were half a dozen bicycles and a huge pile of bundles and boxes.

Not the bus we travelled to Dhumshakti in – another one, equally overloaded.

At one point, the bus stopped while everyone got off the roof, and most of the larger items were offloaded. There was a huge limb of a tree that only cleared the roof of the bus by about nine inches. Then we stopped again while everything and everybody was loaded back on.

In several places, the road crossed watercourses. In each case, this involved a steep descent, an exceptionally rough stretch over rocks and boulders in the stream itself, and then a steep ascent the other side. We had to take these crossings very slowly, so there was no opportunity to get a run up for the climb back up again. The roar of the engine climbing out of the ravines in first gear was something I'll not forget.

That roar is something you learn to recognize. If you're waiting for a bus in a village, you can hear it climbing out of ravines from miles away – it echoes around the mountains. You can learn the specific sound of particular buses in particular ravines, and know when the bus will arrive at your particular stop, twenty minutes or more before it does. This is very useful, because it's impossible for them to keep to their timetable with any accuracy at all, and most of the villagers don't have watches anyway.

The bus ride finished at Rampur, five miles short of Bartola, and we walked those last five miles, a big crowd of us laughing and joking all the way. The sun set before we arrived, but nobody cared. Quite a few people knew the path well enough to find the way by starlight. It was a magical new experience for me.

We arrived to find a meal ready for all of us outside the church. Several oil lamps hanging from poles illuminated the scene. We sat on rafia mats and were waited on by half-a-dozen smiling girls, who served us a delicious chicken curry and rice, in bowls made of huge leaves stitched together with slivers of bamboo. We ate with our fingers. When we'd finished, the girls brought round a jug of water, and we washed our fingers under a trickle of water from the jug.

A few of our number with local connections disappeared off to various houses in the village. The sarpanch (elected village headman, roughly speaking) invited John, Chhoti and Ravi, the guests of honour, to stay at his house. Shanti wanted them to take me too, but I felt awkward about that, and preferred to stay with Shanti and Kamal in the church, where the rest of us were to spend the night.

There were forty odd of us in the church, huddled together on mats, under rajai (sort of cotton wool filled duvet-like things) borrowed for us by Sushila's family from people in the village. Except that it's a single room inside, the church is just like one of the village houses, with mud walls and a roof of half-round tiles on a framework of bamboo and wood that's still recognizably bits of trees.

In the morning, the same smiling girls served a breakfast of sabji (curried mixed vegetables) and puri (oily chapattis, more or less). I was cheeky enough to visit the impromptu kitchen behind the church, where the food was being prepared by a team of lads who looked to be in their twenties. They were cooking on wood fires between rocks, with gharra (huge spherical pottery vessels) and tawa (chapatti skillets) resting on the rocks.

Unlike the girls, who were smartly dressed in what seemed to be their mission school uniforms, the lads were wearing very plain clothes, lungi (wrap around skirts of simple rectangles of cloth) and ragged shirts.

The wedding was in the early afternoon. It was largely a rather serious affair in the church, presided over by an elderly pastor with a very strong voice. He spoke in a dialect so different from the shudh Hindi

I actually took this shot a few years later. This time they were using aluminium cooking vessels.

('pure' Hindi) of Evansganj that I couldn't follow him at all. I could only pick out odd words – apart from when he was reading from the bible, when he read what was written there in plain Hindi.

Ravi and Sushila exchanged silver rings, looking very serious as they put them on each other's fingers.

At the end of the service, three girls appeared with malas (essentially oversize daisy chains but with bigger flowers) and put one on Ravi, and one on Sushila. Then they looked around the church, found me in amongst the ladies on the floor, and came to put one on me. I was sitting next to Chhoti, and tried to get them to put it on her instead, but they weren't having it. It was for me, a visitor from England – even though I did come from Evansganj originally.

Then there was another meal outside Sushila's parents' house, but this time there were about three hundred guests, with all Sushila's family and friends as well as all those from our side.

After the meal, there was a rather formal giving and receiving of wedding presents, with a middle aged man taking a careful record of who gave what. Gifts ranged from a few rupees to a large, handsome metal trunk – into which most of the rest of the gifts were subsequently placed. There was a lot of beautiful bronze kitchenware.

I'd seen that handsome metal trunk on the top of the bus, but it was the sarpanch, not one of our family, who had brought it.

Then some of the lads, some of them those who'd previously been cooking, appeared with drums, and a party began on the field in front of the house. We danced all night by the light of half-a-dozen feeble oil lamps – long lines of us stepping back and forth with our arms around each other's shoulders.

I say we danced all night, and I'm sure some people really did. Every time I saw Uncle John he was in the thick of it.

I danced quite a lot, people laughing good naturedly as I learnt the steps. The only other people as wrong-footed as I was were some of the smaller children, none of whom were sent to bed. They collapsed on their mothers' laps, or any convenient laps, from time to time, but were up again after a little while, and some of them seemed to be dancing as much as any of the adults.

One thing marred the occasion. Grandma was too ill to contemplate the bus ride and the walk, and had had to stay at home. Ayah had stayed in Evansganj to look after her.

Pot luck flash photo. I couldn't see anything through the viewfinder.

The day after the wedding, we all set off for Rampur at first light and caught the early bus back to Dhumshakti. Ravi and Sushila were decked out in their best clothes, and had fresh mala around their necks. Crowded as the bus was, they rode in style, just the two of them on the long sideways-facing seat beside the engine, that would normally be packed with well dressed young men of the kind who have a high opinion of themselves. John, Chhoti and I got special treatment too, with the triple seat just behind the driver all to ourselves.

Nowadays there's a regular bus service between Dhumshakti and Evansganj, but in those days the train was all there was – three trains a day. We knew we wouldn't arrive in time for the scheduled departure of the express from Delhi at one o'clock, but hoped to catch it anyway as it very often ran late.

The Delhi train hadn't yet gone through when we arrived, but the ten o'clock local passenger train turned up at about half past two, and we caught that. Who knew when the Delhi train would actually arrive?

There was no special treatment on the train, but who cares how crowded it is when you're only going ten miles?

We had one day to prepare for Christmas.

Christmas in Evansganj was nothing like Christmas in England. It had changed a bit since the Christmases of my childhood, but not much. The first couple of Lane Christmases in Whitechapel had been more like the old Evansganj Christmases, but we three kids soon learnt about English Christmases from our peers, and Mum and Dad felt obliged to conform.

But by the age of thirty-three I'd learnt to appreciate a less consumerist style. I'm not really a religious person at all – I'm pretty much an atheist – but I don't mind church services, even if they're a bit long-winded. They're very much preferable to an orgy of presents. And the food was better than English Christmas fare, too – really tasty and plenty of it, without being excessive.

It's not that I don't like English Christmas fare; but it would be better to enjoy all the good things over a longer period. It's nearly impossible to refuse each new treat, but you end up eating far too much if you don't. It's not even as though I've got a small appetite – quite the opposite.

I really enjoyed the carol singing in church, and there was lots of it. All the carols were English carols translated into Hindi, sung to a somewhat Indianized version of the English (or German, or other European) tune. In my childhood they'd been sung in English, but that was in the days when Evansganj had a substantial white minority.

Sushila had never been in Evansganj for Christmas before, and said that we should spend Christmas in Bartola some time. A Bartola Christmas is something very different again, but that's another story.

Kamal and Jyoti were married in Jyoti's village, Navadi, on the 27th. I know both Bartola and Navadi quite well now, and know how different they and their people really are, but at the time the two experiences seemed very similar to me – very different from England or Evansganj, in a somewhat similar way. A lot of what I wrote about Ravi and Sushila's wedding could be repeated almost word for word, and to do that seems silly. On the other hand, it seems terrible just to say this wedding was a repeat of the last one!

Even though Grandma still wasn't very well, the easier journey to Navadi meant she felt able to come, and Ayah came too.

One difference was that the Christians in Navadi were a minority, and in particular the sarpanch was a Hindu. He was on perfectly good terms with Jyoti's family, and attended the wedding, but didn't offer his hospitality to anyone. Here again most of us slept in the church, but Grandma, John, Chhoti and Kamal spent the night with one of Jyoti's uncles.

I now know that the dancing in Navadi isn't quite the same as the dancing in Bartola, but at the time I didn't even realize. I just thought I was even more useless at learning the steps than I thought I ought to have been, and put it down to tiredness.

Navadi is actually not very far, as the crow flies, from Bartola; but it's the other side of some very rough jungle country. There are paths, but you need a guide or you could get hopelessly lost. There are deep ravines, steep thickly wooded slopes, rocky ridges and vertical cliffs up or down that you come across unexpectedly in the forest. The paths twist and turn in a most confusing way, even for someone with a good sense of direction. Oh, and there are wild animals: bears, snakes, huge monitor lizards and occasionally tigers or elephants. And bandits. But

Monitor lizard (dead). Uncle John's foot for scale.

it's one of the most beautiful and interesting places I've ever been. The view from the top of the rocks at the highest peak is just amazing. But again, that's another story. I didn't go up there that trip.

Shanti and Peter's wedding was in Evansganj, of course. It was on the 30th, and was very different from either of the others. This was a town wedding, not a village wedding; and it owed a lot more to British influence, not so much because of John and Chhoti and Shanti, but because of the whole Evansganj Indian Christian community. The villages have largely retained their Adivasi (tribal – literally, Aboriginal, and proud to be so) culture, with a veneer of Christianity overlaid on it. Evansganj is still to a considerable extent a remnant of British India, even though it's almost entirely inhabited by people of Indian origin.

A newly arrived Brit might not see Evansganj that way, not until they'd experienced the villages. But the culture in a large part of Evansganj, different as it is from Europe, resembles Europe much more than it resembles the villages.

Not all Indian towns have areas like this, but nor is Evansganj the only one that does, by any means.

On New Year's day almost the whole Evansganj Christian community went for a picnic down by the river. The Christian community? That's an odd way to define the group, but it's hard to know how else one could define it. The outing was organized by the Evansganj Young Christians, but it was open to anyone who wanted to come, and lots of Hindus and Sikhs came along as well.

There were some very Christian Christians in Evansganj, but the majority of the Christian community were about as Christian as the average Brit, and there was no clear dividing line between them and the Hindus or Sikhs, most of whom took their religion about equally casually.

There were a few Christians who, while perfectly friendly with the Hindus, wouldn't attend a Hindu festival, and vice versa; but the majority of people of whichever religion would attend anything that looked like fun.

Sadly, things have changed somewhat – there's a lot more tension between the communities nowadays. Older people used to say intercommunal tension came and went like the tide, but in my admittedly limited experience it's just got worse over the years.

At that time, the Muslim community didn't mix much with the rest, but there was no trouble. In more recent years, some Hindu extremists have caused trouble for both the Muslims and Christians, and while these two groups still don't really mix, there's been a certain amount of co-operation in self defence. It's important to stress that the trouble is caused by a tiny minority – the majority of Hindus are very peaceable people.

Getting back to that picnic! At that time of the year, the river is not much more than a stream in the middle of a wide expanse of sand. A little further downstream, it's mud rather than sand, and the farmers on each side of the river take advantage of the opportunity to grow winter crops in the fertile riverbed; but at Evansganj it's just sand and rocks. Great for a New Year's picnic!

There were plenty of dry sticks in the bushes on the sandbars, where the floods had left them last monsoon. They were just light, hollow sticks of besharam or jamti, not good enough firewood to be worth collecting to take home for cooking, but plenty good enough to make a cheerful blaze on the riverbed. I remembered doing exactly the same thing on New Year's day when I was a little girl.

I'm not really sure how many of us were there, but it can't have been less than a couple of hundred. People had brought all kinds of lovely food, and it was all shared about. Some things were heated up over the bonfire, but mostly it was cold stuff.

Christmas 1981, England

Mr Oldfield heard a noise outside in the garden, and glanced out of the window. There were three lads coming out of the big house, laughing and shoving each other. He knew who they were: they'd been tenants of his in another part of town at one time. What had they been doing in the big house? He was pretty certain they'd been up to no good. They were a rough crowd – racist thugs, as he'd discovered too late when he originally rented a flat to them, and certainly no friends of any of us tenants in the big house.

But they were no friends of his, either, and rough. They seemed to be leaving anyway, and while he wasn't a coward, nor was he a fool. He certainly wasn't going to confront them.

When they'd gone, he went into the big house to see if he could see what they'd been up to. They'd let themselves out through the front door, which could be opened from the inside even when it was locked. Either someone had left it unlocked – unusual – or they'd got in somewhere else. A window left open, perhaps? Or had they broken in somewhere?

It didn't take him long to find out. The door of Flat One, my flat, was swinging open, and inside was a complete mess. They'd broken a window at the back of the house to get in. It looked to him as though their main objective was to trash the place rather than to steal anything, but he couldn't tell – he didn't know what should have been there, and he knew that I was in India at my cousin's wedding, out of contact completely.

The other three flats were untouched.

He rang the police, who came and had a good look, took fingerprints and all sorts. He told them precisely who'd done it. With their permission, he cleaned up the shit (literally) and got a chap to come and repair the window.

I arrived back a couple of weeks later. I was rather upset about some of the things that had been ruined – books, LPs, and photographs particularly – but quite philosophical about it. They'd had it in for me for a while, but that's another story. At least they'd not attacked me bodily.

Somehow the police failed to trace the culprits, although we knew they were around – both Mr Oldfield and I saw them in town from time to time afterwards.

That other story? Since my undergraduate days, I've always been an outspoken opponent of racism.

Well, much earlier than that, really. I spent my first seven years in a poor, puritanical, white protestant Christian community in a small town in India, where the text of the Bible was believed to be literally true in every word. From a very early age I found this idea perfectly unconvincing, despite my being – as far as I knew then – wholly alone in this scepticism.

Most of the community had an unwarranted sense of superiority over their Indian neighbours. Even at six or seven, I was aware of that sense of superiority and how unwarranted it was. That was probably due to Uncle John's influence, although I don't think I was conscious of that at the time. I didn't have any inhibitions about expressing my opinions – at least, not when it was my beloved Ayah who was being abused.

Not that most of the white community thought they were racist. They thought they were virtuously helping the poor Indians by being there, not realizing that their patronizing, condescending attitude was itself racist. But if someone implied that my Ayah would need help with something because she wasn't a clever white person like them, there was a small girl who would loudly and firmly correct their mistake.

Of course Ayah would wisely hush me.

I'm not sure at what stage I learnt to keep my mouth shut, but it might have been on the voyage to London. Maybe it was something the engineer said – he was certainly a big influence on me – but I don't remember. Certainly by the time I went to school in Whitechapel I'd learnt not to speak out unless I was confident of doing more good than harm, and at that stage I wasn't generally very confident.

But as an undergraduate, I found my voice again. I found that I was a bit of an orator, and able to influence my fellow students. I think it helped that I looked, and sounded, like a rather loud eleven year old – and then expressed myself like the articulate young adult that I was.

Almost all the student body was white, but a substantial proportion of the town's population was of Bangladeshi, Pakistani, Indian, or West Indian origin. The National Front were active in the town. Bill, Ben – who is Jewish, albeit not in the least religious – and I stirred up quite a strong opposition to them amongst the students. I was one of the speakers at a lot of meetings, not only in the university, but also in the town.

I received threatening letters, and was shouted at in the street several times, but luckily no-one ever actually attacked me.

We three became friends with the leaders of a mainly Bangladeshi group who'd set up a youth club. Racist thugs had smashed their windows a couple of times. Bill and Ben, who had the necessary tools and skills, replaced the windows for them. The second time, they fitted steel shutters that could be closed every night.

As they were tidying up when they'd finished the job, an old banger passed slowly on the opposite side of the road. The driver opened his window and shouted, "We'll get you!"

Happily this was also a threat that was never carried out, possibly because Bill and Ben are both big, solid chaps, and they were almost always together.

Other people we knew weren't always so lucky.

Some of our friends ran a bookshop. They sold all kinds of books, but specialized in left-wing politics, anarchism, feminism and pacifism. They had an upstairs room that they used as an office, and which they allowed all kinds of radical groups to use for meetings.

Late one evening after a meeting, Mary shut up the shop. We all headed off to our various homes, some on bicycles, many on foot. Bill and Ben lived a little further in the same direction as me, and walked with me as far as my place. Mary lived in the opposite direction, and headed off with a small group who lived that way. Mary's flat was the furthest, but she never got there.

Luckily she was found by a late night dog walker later the same evening; she'd almost certainly have been dead by the morning. She'd been hit over the head, then knifed in the chest and stomach, and left for dead. She was in hospital for six weeks, the first three in intensive care.

Her attackers were never caught.

While she was still in hospital, there was an arson attempt on the shop late one night. Serendipitously, it was foiled when a policeman just happened to pass as a young man was pouring petrol through the letterbox. For once, a known National Front supporter was successfully prosecuted and jailed for three years.

Just a few months later, somebody stole a lorry and reversed it fast into the front of the shop in the middle of the night. The shop was completely demolished. This time the culprits were, as usual, not caught.

Jim and Jane, who'd set up the shop with Mary, were in the process of splitting up by this time. The three of them considered getting new premises, then Mary and Jane considered finding a new partner or two to start a new shop, but nothing ever came of it. I lost touch with all of them after I moved.

OCTOBER 1972

There's another story about Jim, after he and Jane split up but before I left the area.

He was cycling home late one evening. He could hear the noise of fireworks – bangers – and someone laughing, and a child whimpering. The wall on his left angled back sharply away from the road, with a row of derelict shops a few feet further back from the road, waiting to be demolished. As he came past the end of the wall, he saw what was going on. There was a little brown girl cowering in the corner by the last shop, and a scruffy white youth was throwing bangers at her, and laughing.

Jim rode up a low bit of the kerb, and over to them. Neither of them noticed him approaching. He stopped, and put his hand on the lad's arm. The lad turned towards him – and pulled a knife.

Jim couldn't run – he was astride his bicycle. He couldn't cycle off quickly enough, either. He didn't have any time to think, he just reacted. He'd never punched anyone since he was a small child, but he punched that lad – really hard, right under the point of his chin. A lucky instinct, as it turned out.

The lad was a little taller than Jim, but very slightly built. Jim's only medium height, but he's very solidly built – not fat, just solid. As he remembers it – and he admits one's memories of such things can be tricksy, it all happens so fast – the lad lifted right off his feet. He certainly went down like a felled tree, and hit his head on the pavement. He just lay there.

The little girl didn't wait to thank Jim, and he doesn't blame her in the slightest for that. She just ran off.

Jim got on his bike and cycled off, too.

Half a mile down the road, he thought, "I hope I've not killed him." Then he thought, "The street light was behind me. He can't have seen my face at all." Finally, "I'd better go and see if he needs an ambulance. I'll be on my bike, I can leave him behind easily enough if he's up and about and tries to attack me."

By the time Jim got back to the scene, the lad had disappeared, so Jim presumed he'd recovered consciousness pretty quickly and got up with a sore head.

Jim saw him in the centre of town a few days later. Fortunately he didn't show any sign of recognizing Jim.

I know Jim had hit him pretty hard, because he split the skin on his knuckles. I saw it.

Jim never reported the incident to the police. The way the local police force was in those days, he'd probably have ended up being prosecuted for assault.

There was another thing about the time my flat was trashed. Mr Oldfield had told the police who'd done it, and the culprits weren't the kind to have taken great care to avoid leaving fingerprints or other clues. The only possible conclusion I could come to was that the police didn't want to catch them. But if that was the case, why had they taken so much care taking fingerprints, and looking for clues?

Some of my friends concluded instantly that what the police were really after was my fingerprints, and those of my friends. I thought at the time that they were being paranoid, and that the police had probably originally intended to catch the culprits, and only later decided not to bother.

I'm now not so sure. Too many other things have happened to make me much less sanguine about the motivations and behaviour of some parts of the police force. One episode in particular made me think my friends were in fact on more or less the right track. It was actually rather amusing.

Some of my friends were suspicious that the bookshop telephone was being tapped by the police. I was present at the meeting where they decided on a plan, and although I was sceptical, I thought it was a harmless scheme, and went along with it. We prepared an elaborate timetable of telephone calls over a period of a few days, pretending to organize a demonstration that we'd no intention of actually mounting.

It was all very carefully worked out, as though the bookshop was – as it typically was – the hub of the organization, but other telephone calls between third parties were implied by some of the things that were said in the calls to and from the bookshop. The location for this imaginary demonstration was carefully chosen to be within view from the window of Jacob's flat in a tower block, albeit from a considerable distance. We had a couple of pairs of binoculars between us, but we reckoned we'd probably be able to see well enough anyway.

On the appointed day, the police turned up in force. Umm.

Were we guilty of wasting police time? They were scarcely likely to prosecute us for it. On the other hand, it undoubtedly didn't endear us to them, which might not have been the wisest thing we ever did.

But then, wisdom isn't necessarily about maximizing one's own comfort, even one's own long-term comfort.

There was an area of rough ground opposite the bookshop, where an old warehouse had been demolished but nothing had yet been built. It had been levelled, to minimize the risk of injury to children playing there, but it had simply been growing weeds for several years. Then someone bought it and surfaced it and turned it into a car park, charging small sums for people to park there.

One time, the Army booked half of it for a couple of days, for a recruitment drive. They had a few artillery pieces, all nicely polished up, that visitors could actually put their hands on, a caravan covered in camouflage netting, with a recruiting sergeant (or whatever the proper title is) sitting at a desk inside, with leaflets and what-have-you.

The centrepiece of the show was a scaffolding tower supporting a climbing wall, with ropes over pulleys at the top, and big burly soldiers at the bottom. The public were invited to come and climb their climbing wall – or have a go, anyway – with a harness and a nice safe top rope.

We hatched a plot in the bookshop. We had a load of *Troops Out Now* posters, opposing the presence of British troops in Northern Ireland.

Neither Bill nor Ben was available on either of the days this was running, but I was. No-one else in the group of friends involved was a rock climber, and didn't fancy it, although we'd seen plenty of other novices trying it out.

So it was my job. I took off my jumper. Mary pinned a *Troops Out Now* poster on the back of my tee-shirt, and I put my jumper back on. I was ready.

"Can I have a go?"

Harnessed up. Up I went, trying to look as though I wasn't as practiced a rock climber as I really was. Halfway up, there was a gap in the wall where it was fastened to the scaffold tower behind it. I undid the rope from my harness, passed it through the gap, round a scaffold pole, and then reattached it to my harness. Thus safely anchored onto the wall, I calmly removed my jumper, revealing, halfway up the Army's recruitment drive climbing wall, my brightly coloured *Troops Out Now* poster.

Needless to say, the recruiting sergeant had apoplexy. But it took them over an hour to get me down – they couldn't risk doing anything dangerous, so much in the public eye, and of course I wasn't exactly co-operative.

Wise? I'm still not sure. Fun, certainly. Whether it actually influenced anyone, who knows? And if so, in what direction? It hasn't, as far as I can tell, done my career or liberty any harm, which is some consolation. I don't think I'd committed any actual crime that they could charge me with. I guess they didn't think so either, since I was never charged.

The other idea that was bandied about in the bookshop would definitely not have been wise, and fortunately that was recognized by all present at the time. But we had a good laugh talking about it.

One of us was teaching electronics at the local technical college, and his students were making printed circuit boards, using ferric chloride to etch away the copper where it wasn't protected with photoresist. We thought of several ways that a millilitre or two of wet ferric chloride could be introduced into the barrels of the artillery pieces, with minimal risk of the culprit being noticed.

Ferric chloride corrodes steel pretty rapidly (even stainless steel, although that wasn't relevant in this case). It wouldn't make holes right through a gun barrel, but it would wreck the surface of the bore. What fun! But minimal risk isn't zero risk, and this was after 1971 and the passage of the Criminal Damage Act.

I'm pretty sure the damage would have been noticed before anyone attempted to fire the guns, but if not, I'm not sure what the consequences would have been. Whether it would be enough to cause a barrel burst, either by obstructing the bore with corrosion products, or by weakening the barrel, or both, I don't know. A barrel burst in a substantial artillery gun would very likely be fatal for those close to it.

And all to what end? It certainly wouldn't stop any fighting.

December 1990

All three of my cousins – the ones I know about, that is; no-one I know knows anything about Dad's brothers after they left Evansganj, or any families they may have had – were married around Christmas 1981. I'd been to India a couple of times in between, but I didn't spend Christmas in India again until 1990. I asked for and was granted a couple of weeks of unpaid leave from my teaching job, and arrived in India early in December, just before air fares started to rise for the Christmas holiday period.

My two eldest nieces and one nephew were all eight, and there were several younger nieces and nephews. They all climbed all over me, and I'm sure they had a wonderful time. I certainly did.

Ravi and Sushila pressingly invited me to spend Christmas itself in Bartola, with Sushila's family. I unhesitatingly accepted.

Sunday, December 23rd 1990

The bus to Rampur was very crowded, but not nearly as crowded as it had been the first time I'd ridden on that route, when I went to Ravi and Sushila's wedding in 1981. Sushila said it was more crowded than usual, because of people going home to their villages for Christmas. But that's spread over several days, it's not like a whole wedding party added to a single bus. It seemed almost as crowded as before inside, but there weren't so many people on the roof.

The road had improved no end in the intervening nine years. All but one of the watercourses that we'd forded in 1981 now had bridges or culverts, and the one that we still had to ford had a concrete roadway under the water rather than just the natural riverbed. The concrete had obviously been there a few years – it was starting to break up, and the driver had to steer very carefully to avoid a wheel dropping into too deep a hole in the concrete. But it was a lot better than when it had just been jumbled rocks.

As before, we had to walk from Rampur, and as before, it was gone sunset before we arrived in Bartola. This time there were only us three adults and Ravi and Sushila's three children not a whole crowd, but spirits were just as high. With no telephones, and only a slow and unreliable postal service, no-one in Bartola knew we were coming. Sushila's parents assumed Ravi and Sushila and the children would probably come for Christmas, but they'd no idea I was even in India, much less that I'd be spending Christmas in Bartola. But Sushila assured me that I'd be very welcome, and she was right.

Some of the other bus passengers were also from Bartola, and had left their bicycles in Rampur, so word of our impending arrival preceded us by nearly an hour. By the time we arrived, Sushila's parents were waiting for us in front of their house. They had a Petromax – a pressurized paraffin lamp, much brighter than the ordinary lanterns – hanging on the wall by the front door. The house had changed a lot since I'd last been there.

As we came up the path across the field towards the house, Sushila's younger sister Asren ran over to me. She produced a mala from behind

Loading the bus in Dhumshakti. Many passengers arrived by rickshaw. Luggage and bicycles went on the roof – as did some passengers, because the bus was very full.

her back, and practically threw it over my neck before I had a chance to react. How she'd managed to get one together in the short notice she'd had, I'll never understand. I must have blushed scarlet, but by the light of a fairly distant Petromax, no-one can have noticed.

We sat cross-legged, or in various similar postures, on grass matting on the floor, around a wood fire in a corner of a little room off the courtyard. There was a double door to the outside world behind us, and a doorless doorway onto the courtyard beside the fire.

The Petromax was extinguished. The only light was the light of the fire, and over the top of a wall, flickering firelight visible on the underside of the roof above another room, which I learnt was the kitchen. I could hear the sounds of activity in the kitchen, and I could smell the smoke from the fires, and something delicious happening in the kitchen.

The things that had happened in maybe an hour between the arrival of the first cyclist off the bus, and our arrival! Sushila's elder brother Alok had killed, plucked and gutted a chicken, and his wife Anya was cooking it. A fire had been lit and got going nicely in the little room off the courtyard. A mala had been made for me.

Part of the route between Rampur and Bartola. Not actually the same occasion, but what the hell.

I learnt later that the Petromax had been borrowed, as had a khatia – a bed, or charpoy – for me. Why they thought I couldn't sleep on a grass mat on the floor like everybody else, I don't know, but I'd got used to not arguing about things like that. No point hurting people's feelings.

We sat quietly for quite a while, then Sushila's mother began singing softly. Renu – Ravi and Sushila's youngest, just three years old – was nearly asleep on her lap. The little girl looked up at her when she started singing, and smiled. In the firelight they made a wonderful picture that sticks in my mind to this day, but the old film camera I had in those days couldn't have captured it, and I wouldn't have wanted to get it out anyway.

Every now and then Sushila's father put a few more bits of wood on the fire, and every now and then he'd rearrange the fire a bit, poking at it with a piece of metal tube, or blowing on it down the tube to coax some part of it into flame. He didn't actually put the tube to his mouth: he pursed his lips and blew into the tube from half an inch or so away from the end. Of course this drags additional air into the tube, all around the jet from the mouth. Not only does this increase the amount of air you can deliver, it also means that most of it is fresh air, not laden with carbon dioxide and water vapour from the lungs.

Not the party I came with, but no-one knew these relatives were coming, either. A meal was ready for them in short order anyway, although it was well past bedtime.

Presumably for Sushila's father a matter of long experience, not theoretical knowledge!

I only discovered much later that the tube was a piece cut by the local blacksmith from the frame of an old bicycle that was beyond repair. It must have been pretty far gone – it's amazing what can be repaired in Indian villages, where a worker's time doesn't seem to be an issue, and people just seem to get on with things and get them done anyway.

December 24th 1990

I woke before dawn to a strange sound – a regular creak-thud, creak-thud, creak-thud. I couldn't work out what it could possibly be. A child playing trampoline on a bed? Scarcely – I had the only bed in the house, and it wasn't the kind of bed a child could have trampolined on anyway. It went on and on and on. Eventually I went back to sleep with it still going on. I don't know how long it was before I woke again, but it had stopped.

Sushila, Asren and I spent the day making Christmas decorations. We cut hundreds of little triangles of coloured tissue paper out of big sheets Sushila had fetched from Evansganj. We twisted four strands of cotton thread together into a sort of thin string, and stretched it here and there across the courtyard in the middle of the house. Finally we folded one edge of each triangle around the strings, and glued it down with flour and water paste.

Some of them didn't seem to want to stick, but we left those ones to dry for a while and then tried them again. We broke a couple of the strings in the process of sticking on the triangles. We tried to knot them together again, but found we needed to put in an extra bit of string. They wouldn't stretch enough to make a knot without. We'd broken one of them a second time in the attempt.

The whole of the front of the house had been newly whitewashed for Christmas a few days earlier. Asren mixed up a little more whitewash, mixed in a small amount of blue powder pigment Sushila had also brought from Evansganj, and painted a very artistic nativity scene in blue on the white wall. Then she wrote *Happy Christmas*, in English, underneath it, and just to make sure, बारा दिन मुबारक हो underneath that.

This seems to me to be the right moment to describe the house a little. It had grown a little since I'd first visited, nine years earlier, with a new room closing off a courtyard that had previously been open on one side.

The walls of the new room were constructed of bricks, but all the older walls were built of unfired, sun-dried clay. Apart from the fact that the walls of the new room were straighter than the old walls, you'd scarcely have noticed the difference unless you were told – all the walls were plastered regularly with a mixture of fresh mud and cow dung, usually with a little carbolic acid (phenol) mixed in as a disinfectant.

The roof had a framework of round timbers – just tree trunks cut by axe, with the bark and branches removed by adze but not sawn into pieces at all. Bamboo spanned across the rafters, and covering all that were rough tiles.

There was no ceiling in any of the rooms, apart from the one room where there was an upper storey above it. You could see the whole structure of the roof from the underneath.

Going to the loo meant taking a lota – a little pot of water – to wash your backside, and disappearing into the jungle out of sight. At least there was jungle to disappear into. Elsewhere in India, you had to, and still have to, make do with the corner of a field, very likely shared with half a dozen other people on the same mission.

The inside of the roof of Sushila's parents' house. This is what you see looking up from almost any room of any village house.

There was no electricity or running water. Lighting was by paraffin lamp, normally just a storm lantern, but that Christmas there was that borrowed Petromax. Water came in buckets from the well, twenty-five yards from the house.

In the kitchen, cooking was done over a wood fire in a chulha – a clay fireplace with two round holes just too small for the smallest pan to fall through into the fire, and three lumps in the rim so that the pans were lifted slightly, to let the flames come up round the pan.

The smoke simply rose up through the room and went out through the gaps between the tiles. This did mean that the kitchen could be quite smoky.

I don't know why I described all that in the past tense. It's still exactly like that, as are almost all the houses in that area, and in many other areas of India. Navadih has changed a little – it has electricity now! When there isn't a power cut, which is almost every day, often for hours at a time, just when you want it most, in the evenings. When, if ever, electricity will come to Bartola, who knows?

The smoke in the houses results in a significant number of people, particularly women, getting various eye problems (pterygium, entropion, and ectropion particularly); but against that, it gives significant protection against malaria, discouraging mosquitoes especially in the evening when they're most active, and people are most likely to be round the fire.

Cooking on a chulha.

You might think all that makes it sound very primitive. Well, maybe it is. And life is certainly hard in Bartola, but mostly it's not the things I've described here that make it hard. Collecting wood for cooking is hard though, and so is fetching water from the well. Growing almost all your own food, and a little more on top of that to sell to buy clothes, tea, sugar, spices (other than those you grow yourself), paraffin, soap, tools and so forth – that's what's *really* hard. Not so bad for those families where someone, or a few people, have jobs, and can contribute a little money; but they usually expect to get at least a proportion of their food from home, too.

All that said, it's a better life than the life of the poor in the cities. So why do poor people migrate from the countryside to the cities?

In some cases, it's because they mistakenly think the streets of the cities are metaphorically paved with gold. In a few cases, they're not even mistaken, and they do manage to carve out a comfortable niche for themselves in the cities – but in most such cases, it's a mistake.

But most migrants never thought that in the first place – they don't choose to go to the cities, they're forced to. Sometimes that's due to population growth – their parents' land is divided between all the

Smoke from a chulha rising through the tiles of a village house. Notice the solar panel (bottom right) – this village doesn't have electricity. The solar panel charges a battery than runs a television for about two hours in the evening, before the battery goes flat. The picture is not good. The village is theoretically beyond the reach of the transmitter, and the aerial – atop that bamboo pole above the solar panel – is not wonderful.

brothers, and the resulting plots are simply too small to support them. But very often there would be enough land, if it wasn't for land-grabbing by the rich and powerful, who want to build a huge dam to irrigate their own huge farms downstream, or to mine for bauxite, iron ore, or coal, or to make a plantation to grow cash crops – possibly for export, and possibly jatropha, a horribly poisonous plant grown to make biodiesel.

You think you're doing India a favour when you buy Indian produce? You might be doing the Indian middle classes a favour, giving them foreign currency to buy the latest technological gadget – but you might very well be doing the Indian poor a disfavour.

Exactly what the Catholics of Bartola do on Christmas night, I don't know. Like about a third of the population of Bartola, Sushila's family are protestant, and belong to the Church of North India.

Sometime probably a little before midnight, we all trooped off to the church. We sat on grass matting inside. All the women, girls, and smaller children sat on the left of the church, and all the men and bigger boys on the right, with a clear gangway down the middle. The same pastor who'd married Ravi and Sushila delivered a relatively short sermon and read a short passage from Luke, Chapter I. Then we sang several Christmas carols from the same hymn books we'd sung from in Evansganj – except that these were an older edition, and they were falling to bits whereas the Evansganj ones were in pretty good condition.

The singing was a little different, too. It was still the same translations of the European carols, and still recognizably the same European tunes. The pronunciation of the Hindi was noticeably different – more like the sound of the local village language, although the words were all the Hindi words, not the local ones. And the singing sounded very like other, non-religious Bartola Adivasi singing, which sounds very unlike Europeans singing – yet the tunes were still perfectly recognizably *Silent Night*, *O Little Town of Bethlehem* and so on.

And Evansganj church has an organ, but the carol singing in Bartola was unaccompanied.

It was probably about half past one in the morning by the time we got to bed.

CHRISTMAS DAY, 1990

Despite the late night, we were up not long after dawn – to the sound of drumming, the tinkle of dozens of little bells, and cheerful singing. A group of young men were in the courtyard, dancing and singing and beating the drums that hung around their necks. One of them was wearing a broad leather belt with a couple of dozen little bells that jingled as he danced. Most were barefoot, but one had a pair of old boots that seemed three sizes too big for him – and no socks. Thud, thud, thud they went on the bare earth of the courtyard.

Well – not exactly bare earth. Once a week or so it got a fresh coat of cow dung, which is mixed with a little carbolic acid and enough water to make a good slurry for spreading, and which dries to a better surface than bare earth.

Everybody was up and about within minutes, and all the children joined in the dancing. Anya, who had anticipated this, soon appeared with leaf-bowls of rice and chicken curry for the visitors – very small portions, because they'd be visiting all the Protestant households in the immediate neighbourhood within the hour!

Bartola is like many villages in the area, in that most of the houses are scattered over a large area, with just a few clustered together in the centre. Neither of the two churches – one Catholic, one Protestant – is

in the centre of the village. I learnt that there were three groups of young men in Bartola who would be doing the rounds that morning, each covering about a third of the village.

The young men departed, and we sat down to breakfast in the little room by the courtyard. It was a special breakfast – chilka roti, a sort of flat, course rice flour crumpet; idli, little rice cakes steamed in little dishes rather like egg poachers; and chicken curry.

I say "we sat down to breakfast", but it wasn't all of us. Asren, Sushila, and Anya served the rest of us, but they themselves ate later, in the kitchen.

There's no present giving as such in Bartola, but working in Evansganj, Sushila and Ravi had more money than the rest of the family, and had brought new clothes for everyone. They'd given them out as soon as we'd arrived, but nobody put them on until after breakfast on Christmas morning, ready to go to church at midday.

Outside the church, the young men with drums started playing them again, and the rest of us joined arm in arm in long lines and danced

and danced and danced – stepping back and forth in the same way we'd danced at Ravi and Sushila's wedding all those years before.

The sermon and reading were somewhat longer than they'd been in the middle of the previous night, and we must have sung just about every carol in the book. The smaller children got very restless, but no-one minded them playing around everyone's feet while we all stood and sang, or even chasing each other around the church laughing and shouting. Their noise couldn't compete with the singing anyway.

The church was decorated in the same fashion as the courtyard at the house – little triangles of coloured tissue paper glued onto threads strung across from roof beam to roof beam. There was a Christmas tree of sorts alongside the altar rail. It wasn't a pine tree, which don't grow around Bartola, but a small tree with waxy oval leaves, of a variety I didn't recognize. (Years later I did see pine trees growing in India, at Mussoorie. But that's a very long way from Bartola.)

Renu spent half the time we were in church removing leaves from the Christmas tree. Nobody interfered with this activity. She was totally

absorbed, inspecting the leaves closely. Later on she showed me one very proudly. It had intricate patterns of leaf miner tunnels in it.

Then we all sat outside the church on grass mats, chatting and playing games – no, not board games or card games! Games with handfuls of small stones, or just voices and bare hands.

One favourite with the smaller children is *Machili, Machili, Beng* – fish, fish, frog. One player waves a finger, imitating a fish swimming in the river, and shouting *Machili, Machili*; the other, the fisherman, suddenly grabs for it, but if the first player is quick enough, the fisherman ends up with the first player's thumb – a frog – in their grasp, not the fish, as the first player shouts *Beng!* It reminds me a little of *scissors, paper, rock;* a similar level of amusement, albeit with very different rules. Ravi, who is full of fun, sometimes plays a trick, grabbing the fisherman instead of sticking up his thumb, and shouting *Mugger!* – crocodile.

People told stories – some old, some new, some basically just the current gossip. There's no clear dividing line between this week's gossip, last year's gossip, and stories going back generations. I heard a lot of stories about the missionaries who'd lived in a village a few miles away, who'd been gone twenty years earlier. Some people

Stitching leaves together with slivers of bamboo to make bowls and plates.

thought they'd been saints; some, even among these Christians, had a very different view of them. There was no rancour about the disagreements though. Everyone laughed about each other's viewpoints.

Several young men started cooking a communal meal on wood fires between stones supporting the pans, and several older women started making bowls out of large leaves, stitching them together with slivers of bamboo. It was getting dark by the time the bowls and the food were ready, and people began lighting lanterns. I noticed that nobody had brought Petromaxes – it was all storm lanterns.

Leaf bowls and plates in use. Midnight feast at the wedding.

DECEMBER 26TH 1990

I was woken before dawn again, by the same creak-thud, creak-thud, creak-thud. I was puzzled, but guessed it was something pretty normal, and it was somehow quite a soothing sound really. I considered getting up and investigating, but felt too cosy in my bed. I snuggled down and went back to sleep.

In 1990, it wasn't yet possible to book berths in Indian trains from anywhere except the station where you were going to start the journey. Each station had a quota of reservable berths on each train. If you couldn't get a reservation, you could board the train and find the TTI (train ticket inspector). He might be able to find you a berth that hadn't been used from an earlier station's quota – particularly if you knew roughly how much to offer him as an incentive.

That's corruption, of course – but not of a kind that I find terribly objectionable. TTIs don't earn a high salary, the bribes they take aren't big, and the people who pay them are comfortably off. People who can't afford to pay those bribes are not disadvantaged in any very important way by their inability to pay.

The kind of corruption that really gets my goat is things like bureaucrats refusing to register villagers' payment of their land taxes without substantial kickbacks. The bureaucrats are very much better off than the people from whom they're extorting money, who often are kept virtually – or completely – destitute by their oppressors.

Back to the TTI's little scam. I knew all those kinds of trick well enough by 1990, but it's chancy, especially at busy times. There may genuinely be no untaken berths, and then you have to travel in the very crowded unreserved compartments. I prefer second class to first, but unreserved really is dreadful at busy times. The people are nice enough, but the sheer physical crush of bodies and luggage is a bit much.

You can even serve tea in leaf bowls. Yes, really. Not too hot, please.

The ticket office at Evansganj only opened from an hour before a train was due to depart until half an hour after it actually departed. This sometimes meant that it was open most of the day, but occasionally there were days when all six trains ran on time, and some of them were due within twenty minutes of each other, so on those days the ticket office wasn't open all that much.

Foolishly, I hadn't reserved my return to Delhi when I first arrived. Only after we arrived in Bartola did we discover that one of Sushila's cousins was going to get married on January 1st. Everyone wanted to stay in Bartola.

I needed to get that reservation. I decided to get the bus and the train, back to Evansganj on the 27th of December, reserve my berth, and then come back to Bartola in time for the wedding. That meant getting up very early to catch the first bus in Rampur at six o'clock – if I caught a later bus, I wouldn't be able to get back the same day.

Sushila promised to wake me in time to get some breakfast, and then she'd walk with me to Rampur. I was confident of finding my way okay, but she insisted.

December 27th 1990

I was woken by the creak-thud again, before Sushila came to wake me. This time I did get up to go and investigate, since I was going to have to get up very soon anyway. My watch said twenty-five past four.

I soon found the source of the noise. I'd never been round the back of the house before. There was an open veranda, and under it was a strange device – well, actually two, but I didn't discover what the other one was for until much later.

It was like a heavy, asymmetrical see-saw made out of a tree trunk pivoted about a third of the way along. The long end was thick and heavy, with a stout piece of wood jammed at right angles to it through a hole bored in it. The stout piece of wood had a thick iron ring round the bottom end. The shorter end was thinner, but equally wide.

I later learnt this device was called a *dheki*.

Anya was standing at one end of the dheki, carrying Renu in a sling and holding onto a pole to brace herself. With one foot she was repeatedly pressing on the short, flattened end of the dheki, lifting the other end up and dropping it again.

The iron-shod crosspiece went thud, thud, thud down into a hole in the floor. (It has a cup made of a very hard wood in the bottom, but I couldn't see that then). Sushila's mother's hand shot in and out of the hole between thuds, scooping rice out of the hole into a sort of open-sided basket – a *supa*, I later learnt. While the thudding continued without a break, she poured some more rice – still in its husks – into the hole. Then she picked up the supa, and tossing the rice up and back, up and back, up and back, she separated the polished rice from the husks, the husks falling on the floor and the rice staying in the supa.

She tipped the rice into a vessel, and started scooping out the next batch.

Since then, I've learnt to work the dheki myself, but only the standing up, foot thumping end. I need a child in a sling like Anya had, or a large stone, because like Anya, I'm not heavy enough to do it otherwise. Ravi can do it without.

The other end is quite a skilled job, and I've never dared try – it looks only too easy to end up with your hand getting crushed under the iron-shod crosspiece. Even at the foot end you have to be careful to keep a regular rhythm, so the person at the other end can avoid getting their hand crushed.

I've tried the supa tossing thing to separate rice and husks, but I've not managed to get the knack. You can separate all kinds of things in the same fashion, once you have the knack.

It takes a long time for two people to polish a day's worth of rice for a large family, using a dheki. You can still hear that creak-thud sound in the pre-dawn all over rural India – although there are nowadays more powered rice polishing machines around, sometimes electric, sometimes driven by a stationary diesel engine, sometimes driven by a tractor. There isn't one in every home, even where everybody is growing their own rice – but many people have a little money, enough to pay the folks who have the machine – or sometimes they'll pay for the polishing with a small fraction of the rice. Every home used to have its own dheki, and most still do, even if it's only used when the money's running low.

Although I didn't learn until much later what the other device was, I'll describe it now. It's a *patni*, an oil press (not to be confused with *patni*, wife, which has a different T – dental, not palatal).

It consists of two lengths of timber supported on two short posts at a low table level, the lower one fixed and the upper one free to slide up and down the posts, which pass through holes near its ends. At one end, the timbers are lashed together, and at the other end, a third, lighter and shorter timber is lashed down close to the main two, and passes over the upper timber at right angles, forming a system of levers. Someone pressing down on the end of this third timber can thus apply a very large force squeezing anything placed between the middle of the main timbers.

Nuts or seeds from which oil is to be extracted are ground to a powder using the dheki, and steamed over a wood fire on the chulha. The steamed powder is placed in a split bamboo basket, woven diagonally so that it can stretch and compress vertically, and pressed in the patni. Oil – for cooking, or for oiling the skin or hair – trickles out, guided by channels carved in the upper surface of the lower timber of the patni, into a pan beneath.

Like the dheki, hard work. At least you don't have to do it so often. More and more people nowadays grow the oil seed and sell it, then buy factory-pressed oil, saving themselves a lot of work but losing a fair amount in the exchange and risking getting inferior quality oil. In particular, they're constrained in which seeds they can sell and what kinds of oil they can buy.

The very best oil, mustard oil (it really is the best, not just in flavour, but nutritionally), was banned in India for a considerable period, and in the USA and EU can still theoretically only be sold for non-food uses. This is a scandal of major proportions. But you can read about that elsewhere (see APPENDIX I).

Sushila called me for breakfast before her mother and Anya had finished polishing the day's rice. We ate quickly, and then set off for Rampur. Sushila made sure I was safely on the bus before she set off back to Bartoli.

The whole area is a bit lawless. It's well known for it, within India if not, at that time, by the British Foreign Office. Life is full of risks, some bigger, some smaller. You can't avoid them. I try to avoid the bigger risks, but I'm not going to live a pointless existence in cotton wool. People sometimes get killed by Naxalites (armed revolutionaries) or dacoits (bandits). But not often.

Well, not more than once. Joking aside, it's a real risk, but a small one, and I don't worry about it. It's probably a bigger risk for me, with the white skin that shouts "Money!" in India, but it's still not a big one.

But on the way back to Bartola, the bus was held up by gunmen. Dacoits, or Naxalites? They said they were Naxalites, but bandits can say that if they think it's to their advantage. Either type of gunman is after the same thing: money. Either to fund their lives, or to fund their revolutionary activities.

The boundary between Naxalites and dacoits isn't necessarily always a clearly defined one anyway. Many of the Naxalites are only members of the group for what they can get out of it for themselves, and so are not much different from other dacoits pretending to be Naxalites. Either is liable to summary execution by genuine, or more committed – or rival – Naxalites, but fear of that possibility doesn't always stop them.

Be all that as it may, two gunmen stood inside the front of the bus, watching everybody, while a third walked calmly down the bus demanding everybody's money. The bus conductor meekly handed over all the takings, and almost everybody turned out their pockets.

Some of the well-dressed young men on the long seat by the engine had to be reminded that they didn't keep all their money in one pocket, but they didn't argue much.

I didn't have to be reminded. I keep most of my money in a bag hanging round my neck, under my kameez, relatively safe from pickpockets in Delhi or on the major stations, but I knew better than to pretend I didn't have more than was in the side pocket of my kameez. I handed over the six hundred rupees I had in my bag, together with the forty-odd rupees I had in my pocket. It was a lot of money at that time, probably more than the total of what everyone else on the bus had.

But it left me with absolutely nothing – not even the bus and train fares back to Evansganj. I knew that the other members of my party were unlikely to have much more than their own fares.

Everything had seemed very calm and polite. I took a chance. I was pretty sure it wouldn't work, but I was also pretty sure it wouldn't have serious consequences.

"How can I get back to Evansganj now? I don't have any money at all!"

The gunman turned to his colleagues at the front of the bus. One of them gestured in a way I wasn't sure I understood, but obviously my gunman did. "How much are the fares?"

"Four rupees on the bus, and two-fifty on the train."

He calmly counted out six rupees and fifty paise and gave it to me. "Have a nice day," he said. In English. His face and his tone of voice said he meant it, too. There wasn't a trace of irony.

While it's true there's a continuum between outright dacoits and committed Naxalites, there really is an important distinction between the two. The Indian élite don't like you to make the distinction, but then they don't like you to draw the parallels between the outright dacoits and the Indian élite, either. For the ordinary Adivasi villager – and probably the ordinary Dalit (lower caste) villager too, for that matter, but I don't know any of them very well – the Indian élite are a much bigger threat than the dacoits, never mind the Naxalites.

That's not to say that I approve of the Naxalites, I don't. But the dacoits are worse, and the élite are worse again. In principle, the Naxalites are on the villagers' side, which is more than can be said for either dacoits or the élite.

In practice, the Naxalites usually do more harm than good, with the villagers getting caught in the crossfire, literally or metaphorically.

Villagers often get mistaken for Naxalites by the police. This is understandable, since the Naxalites are often villagers who happen to be Naxalites, and who are consequently indistinguishable from villagers when they don't choose to identify themselves as Naxalites. Of course there are also policemen who are villagers who are Naxalites, and educated youths from wealthy families who are Naxalites, and so forth – yet somehow those facts don't seem to result in so many police errors.

Sometimes educated people doing social or medical work amongst the Adivasi villagers find themselves in conflict with the bureaucrats and senior police who are extorting money or grabbing land from the villagers, and then they may well be branded as Naxalites – but they aren't usually shot dead in fake "encounters", although they may end up in very unpleasant jails for extended periods.

Naxalites sometimes mistake villagers for police informers, usually with fatal results. And of course Naxalites largely rely on villagers for their money and food, sometimes given freely but more often demanded at the point of a gun. Again, this occasionally has fatal results.

The distinction between "sometimes", "occasionally" and "often" is important. Naxalites are dangerous, dacoits more so, but the police are very much more dangerous than either. Naxalites and dacoits are a drain on the villagers' resources, but the police are a bigger drain, and the bureaucrats are a bigger drain still.

Dacoits have no redeeming features at all, but Naxalites do. In my opinion, it doesn't anywhere near make up for their bad side, but there's no (reasonable) denying their good side.

Such justice as there is in these areas is administered by the Naxalites. It's rough justice, with no guarantee that the judgements will be fair, and often with harsh penalties for those judged to be guilty. But it's usually better, from the ordinary man or woman's point of view, than the official judicial system.

For example, outside Naxalite areas, if a rich youth rapes a poor girl, he will almost certainly get off scot free. The girl wouldn't usually be stupid enough to go to the police, who, even if she was very lucky and they believed her and cared, would know there was no chance of getting a conviction. There's even a significant risk that she'd get raped by one or more policemen. In a Naxalite area, the rich youth would be very unlikely to dare to rape a poor girl.

When a man is killed, either by the police or by the Naxalites or dacoits, the Naxalites generally make sure that his wife and family are looked after. Officially, there is a system for the state to do the same, with "gratuities" paid to the families – when they're actually paid. Very often by the time the legitimate beneficiary turns up, someone else impersonating them has already collected the money – or so the bureaucrat in charge says. Possibly it's sometimes even true.

Even when the gratuities are paid out, they're little enough compensation for the loss of a breadwinner, much less for the loss of a protector. And that's before you begin to think about love and grief.

I've talked with committed Naxalites. They recognize that in the short term, all their good work is generally outweighed by the bad consequences of what they and their hangers-on do. Where they and I differ is that they believe that in the long run, their activities will change the system for the better. I don't see it.

Uncle John is well known in the area, and to a lesser extent I've become so too. The senior Naxalites know who we are, and generally approve of us. Nowadays, I don't feel in personal danger from them or from most of the local Naxalites. But dacoits, dacoits posing as Naxalites, and some of the less well disciplined Naxalites – well, there's no denying they pose a hazard.

But not a huge one. The perilous nature of Indian traffic is pretty certainly a far, far bigger one.

This chap arrived on his bicycle and asked if there were buckets needing mending. Sushila told me that he lives in a village about twelve miles away from Bartola, and that he'd undertake a wide range of light metalwork, but that buckets are his bread and butter.

I suppose you'd call him a tinker. He's a highly skilled tinker. He's also a very nice, friendly, straightforward and perceptive chap.

The hole in this bucket wasn't making it completely useless, but it did mean that you had to transfer the water into some other container as soon as you'd pulled it up out of the well. After he'd repaired it, you could leave a bucketful standing by the side of the well and it would still be there an hour or two later.

While he was mending this bucket, he spotted a couple of brass hand-pump parts lying about, and asked if they were scrap. They weren't really scrap. They'd been bought to repair a pump that proved to be beyond repair. The new parts were perfectly good; but it wouldn't have been worth the bus fares to take them back to the place where they'd been bought, and they might not have taken them back anyway.

So he took them away with him, saying he'd make something out of them. He came back a couple of days later with the things he'd made – a display of craftsmanship that he doesn't get the chance to exhibit every day.

He'd made a couple of rice measuring vessels: one filling of uncooked rice for each person you're cooking for. He said they'd hold 250g of rice – and they really do. Exactly.

"How did you do it? Who taught you how to do it?"

"I can't tell you how I did it. God taught me."

In other words, he invented (some of) his techniques himself, and has developed them over many years.

Watching and listening to Anya haggling with him over the price to pay for those rice measurers was fascinating. Almost embarrassing for someone with pounds in her pocket, but I've got used to the fact that I mustn't distort the local market more than is inevitable. Suffice it to say that she paid well under a pound for the pair. She'd supplied the brass, of course – but he did the work.

They were both very respectful and dignified about the whole procedure, which took about ten minutes.

Civilization is a weasel word – its sneaks an assumption into people's minds. It comes with two meanings, and consequently people associate the two ideas without thinking about it.

The first meaning is this: a way of organizing society on a large and complex scale, with people over a large area, typically many of them in towns and cities, all part of the same large society – as distinct from tribal society, which is somewhat more simply organized on a smaller scale. The second meaning is this: people being well-behaved towards one another.

The consequence of the association in people's minds is that people have the idea that people in societies organized on a large scale are well-behaved, and that people in societies organized on a small scale aren't. This simply isn't true, but it can be quite hard to dislodge the prejudice from people's minds.

I'm not saying that all savages are noble, just that they're as likely to be noble as anyone else – and conversely, civilized people are as likely to be savage as anyone else.

There's another weasel word: savage. Does it mean violent, or does it mean a person belonging to a less complex society? Neither necessarily implies the other!

May 1982

On dry, windless days, one of my regular habits during my research years was to sit on that bench in the park with my lab notebook, a pad of writing paper, and a pen. Sometimes I did some work, and sometimes I just sat there and thought, or wrote something for the local 'alternative newspaper' – an occasional left wing publication put together by a few friends and sold around the town in modest numbers.

One warm Wednesday afternoon I was sitting there, actually working on a paper for a journal – a report of some work I'd been doing – when who should turn up but the same gent who four years earlier had suggested I visit India. He sat down beside me and said, "Well, did you visit India?" Just like that, as if it was only a few weeks since we'd been sitting there before.

"Twice now, actually, I went for the second time last Christmas. Thanks very much for the suggestion!"

We got chatting, and one thing led to another, and we ended up going to the theatre together that Saturday evening. That was the first of many such occasions.

His name was Greg. He was forty-five, I was thirty-three. He'd been a teacher, but had found it very stressful and after a nervous breakdown and a period of unemployment he'd got a job as a counter clerk in a bank. That was two or three years before the first time we met.

A couple of years after we'd first met, his wife had died in a car crash, and he'd been living alone since then.

I visited his flat a few times. Despite damp walls, draughts and inadequate heating, it was clean and tidy, and he was a much better cook than me. He was making the best of a horrible place. It wasn't long before I felt confident enough of him, and I told him to give up the flat and move in with me. My flat was plenty big enough for both of us, and far nicer than his.

We had nine very happy years together. When my university work dried up, I did a postgraduate certificate in education, and started teaching maths and physics in a school quite close to my flat – our flat as I was calling it by then, although it was always in my name.

I say nine happy years, but the last was tinged with sadness. Greg was diagnosed with cancer of the liver. It was too far advanced for surgery, and we were told that he probably had about three months to live. In the event he lived six months. He was fifty-four when he died. He wasn't even a heavy drinker – scarcely drank alcohol at all, particularly after moving in with teetotal little me.

We never had any children. I think he was afraid of the responsibility, but we never actually even discussed it. I think neither of us realized until it was too late that the union was until death did us part.

We'd never married. It had never seemed relevant. It would have been quite funny to be Dr Penny Farthing though.

He'd never been to India with me, either. I was in India – Christmas 1990 – when his cancer was diagnosed. Every time I went, we said that he should come with me "next time." Ho hum.

We did get to Iceland, Greenland, the Faroe Islands and several parts of western Europe together though.

I particularly remember his discovery of trolls – not the obnoxious internet clods who hide behind their supposed (and possibly actual) anonymity in order to harass other users and obstruct discussions, but the kind that originate in Scandinavian myths and legends. We spent some time in a lovely bookshop in Tórshavn in the Faroes, and he was so taken with the children's books about trolls that he bought a few.

That was the point at which I realized Greg should have taught in a primary school, not a secondary school. He loved children, and was good with younger children, but he found teenagers hard to cope with.

We drove all round Iceland in my old Land Rover, and almost wherever we went, Greg saw trolls – stone faces or whole chunky bodies in the rocks and cliffs. He realized that they really were

Icelandic trolls.

troublesome creatures who threw rocks down mountainsides, endangering travellers; and he saw how they moved.

You never actually see them move, but you can tell that they do, because one moment they're not there, and the next, there they are – and then a moment later they're gone again. It's really the mist, one moment hiding them, the next silhouetting them against a backdrop of mist, and then letting them disappear again, camouflaged against a background of more distant rocks.

And they really do throw rocks down at unsuspecting travellers. Rocks certainly come tumbling down dangerously from the crags where the trolls live, anyway.

And the one in the Billy Goats Gruff story, who lived under a bridge, was a distinctly eccentric troll. What a very strange place for a troll to live! They mostly live amongst the rocky crags high in the hills.

I've still got those Faroese children's books, and some that he bought in Iceland, too. I thought about giving them to Pippa's children after Greg died, but they're all written in Faroese and Icelandic, and anyway all my nieces and nephews – and now my great nieces and nephews – love to have them to look at when they visit me. I have toys and games in the house for the same reason.

I remember that bookshop in Tórshavn for another reason. It's one of many buildings in the Faroes that has a turf roof, and I've got a photograph of it that Greg took. I've got a lot of his photographs, but distressingly few of him.

He had a thing about waterfalls, too – especially waterfalls you can walk round behind. Well, truth to tell, so do I.

Iceland has some wonderful waterfalls. You can walk right round behind Seljalandsfoss, and we did. Greg dropped his lens cap there. There was no way we could retrieve it, as it had gone right into the plunge pool.

We drove back into Reykjavik to try to get a new one. It would have been hopeless trying to keep his lens clean otherwise. It's only about ninety miles, but in those days the road was pretty rough, and even in the Land Rover it took a good four hours, and the shops were closing when we got there.

We stayed the night in a youth hostel, which was actually a school during term time, and a youth hostel in the summer. The following day we tried to find a lens cap of the right size. Quite early on, we found a cardboard tube with plastic end plugs that fitted quite well, and bought that. We spent most of the rest of the day trying to find the right lens cap, without success.

Greg's camera sported that plastic end plug as a lens cap to the end of his days – it still does, although the camera hasn't been used since he died. It was actually more satisfactory than the original lens cap, which was too easy to knock off accidentally.

View from behind Seljalandsfoss.

The next best waterfall we knew to walk behind is Hardraw Force, near Hawes in Yorkshire. It's in a lovely glade behind a hotel, through which you have to go to get to the waterfall, and where you have to pay. I remember when the hotel was more a pub than a hotel. I've a feeling that it was run by two old ladies, but I'm not very sure about that. Whoever it was, somehow I didn't mind paying them, it just felt right. The money was certainly going into the local community.

Nowadays the hotel has been developed into something much larger and more modern, and is owned by some national – or even international – chain or other. Somehow it doesn't seem right that they should charge for access to the waterfall. Not that I can justify that feeling – well, not more than I can justify a feeling that national and international chains and corporations are just plain wrong somehow, anyway.

FEBRUARY 1993

One of the good things about moving from teaching into industry was the holidays – I could take them at a time to suit me, instead of having to take school holidays, mostly in Summer. Summer holidays are no good for going to India – they coincide exactly with the monsoon! Anyone would think it was a conspiracy to prevent teachers or schoolchildren visiting India.

In fact, Pericor were so pleased about me not wanting to take my holidays in summer, that they let me take all my '92 and '93 holidays in one lump in February and March '93 – and allowed me to take an extra two weeks unpaid leave at the same time.

It was the first time I'd had a good long visit to India since '78-'79. I did a bit of travelling around India again, this time taking two of my cousins' children with me. We had a wonderful time. I'll come back to that later.

Of course I spent a fair bit of time in Evansganj, too – and in Bartola, where I stayed with Sushila's family for nearly two weeks. Sushila and her children came with me for the first couple of days, then went back home to Evansganj, leaving me in Bartola.

Sushila had told me that I could give small amounts of money to her parents, and to her younger brothers and their wives, by slipping a note into their hands when shaking hands – but that I shouldn't give too much, say ten rupees to the men, and five to the women. I was slightly put out by the idea that I had to discriminate in this way, but held my peace. Sushila knew better than I did what was, and what was not, possible in the way of nudging the culture in what I considered a good direction. By then I'd spent enough time with Sushila to know that she and I had very similar views on this subject!

I wondered how I could really repay her family for my visit, and she and I worked out together that the best thing would be for me to buy myself a bicycle in Evansganj. I would take it on the bus to Bartola with me, use it as long as I was in Bartola, then leave it there "to use next time I visit" – but with instructions that Sushila's parents could use it as much as they liked whenever I wasn't there. Although it would never be actually explicit, they would know that effectively it was their bicycle, with the added protection that they'd be looking after it for me, and that therefore it wouldn't be available for all and sundry to borrow. They had had a bicycle years before. Nobody had actually stolen it, but their four sons had very thoroughly worn it out.

It gave me a wonderful sense of freedom to have a bicycle in Bartola. I cycled all over the place.

I should say something about Indian bicycles here. These days, you do see a few modern bicycles in India, with fancy gears and sprung forks and straight handlebars and very fat tyres – or with drop handlebars and very thin tyres. All the variations you see in Europe or America.

But most bicycles in India are still the old fashioned "sit up and beg" style, with no gears and no suspension. They do often have deeply sprung saddles! They almost all have a strong pannier carrier on the back – for the rider's wife to ride side-saddle on. No springs for her, just some folded cloth. And, very likely, a couple of small children on her knee – and maybe a bigger one sitting astride the crossbar in front of his Dad, too, with a bit of cloth wrapped round the crossbar as a tiny bit of cushioning.

These old fashioned bicycles are *always* black. And they are *strong*. They need to be – to carry the whole family, and on Indian roads at that. At best, Indian roads are full of potholes and covered in quite large loose stones. (On major routes, on bigger roads in cities, and in wealthy areas, this is no longer true. But even in places like that, it was still largely the case in 1993 – and it's still true today everywhere else.)

Not having gears is part of the strength of these bicycles. You'd think a mountain bike would be what you need for these conditions – if you didn't know any better. A mountain bike wouldn't stay the course. The gears and brakes just aren't robust enough. Oh, absolutely lovely for the first year or two. But Indian villagers expect to use their bikes for donkey's years – day in, day out, with little or no attention. They don't want to be cleaning grit out of complicated, oily gear mechanisms every other day. And they certainly wouldn't even consider paying anyone else to do it for them.

Around Bartola, there aren't really any roads in the modern sense at all – more like rough mountain tracks. A couple of them are wide enough for a jeep, but so rough that even a jeep can only negotiate them extremely slowly and with great care. Mostly they're only fit for pedestrians and animals – and cyclists. With no gears, the family have to get off and walk up anything more than a gentle gradient, while Dad rides as far as he can before he too has to get off and push. Then he waits at the top for the family to catch up.

You can't go more than about twelve or at most fifteen miles an hour on the flat – you simply couldn't keep up with the pedals. Most people tend to do about eight. Downhill, of course, you can go as fast as you feel safe – or faster if you're not too worried about safety, or haven't thought about it.

One route I cycled just about every day was back and forth between Bartola and Rampur. There was a market in Rampur, and various shops. Absolutely fascinating – totally different from the market and shops in Evansganj, with totally different stock, totally different pricing, and altogether a totally different attitude to life.

I remember when I first arrived in Delhi, it seemed like a completely different world from England. I remembered my own childhood in Evansganj a little, but it was rather vague and dreamlike. Delhi was real – and different. Then, when I returned to Delhi after a few weeks in Evansganj, it seemed more like an outpost of Europe than part of India.

After a few days in Bartola, one realizes that Rampur and Bartola are the real India – and Evansganj itself isn't really very different from Delhi, or even Europe.

I got to know every rut and pothole on the route between Bartola and Rampur, and exactly how to thread my wheels between them to optimize my ride. I flew back and forth along that route at breakneck speed, in a manner quite unlike any of the locals. Of course I didn't have three or four passengers or a quintal of rice on my panniers – but not all of them did, either. Possibly more importantly, maybe I didn't have their laid back attitude to life. Or maybe I was just used to the speeds at which I could easily ride a bicycle back home.

I rapidly got a reputation as the mad cyclist.

Just before Rampur, the track from Bartola joins a bigger track that actually carries some motorized traffic. Not a lot. Only jeeps and big trucks and buses can negotiate it. You couldn't drive an ordinary car along there, but it's a road of sorts. Just after that, there's a place where the road fords a small river. I'm told that it's impassable in the monsoon, but it's easily forded for the rest of the year. The bottom is sandy, and that's hard going on a bike.

Most people get off and walk through there. I learnt how to take a run at it – exactly where to put my wheels amongst the ruts and potholes down the steep descent into the ravine the river runs in. I was going fast enough to make it across before I ran out of momentum, and still going fast enough at the other side to get up out of the ravine again without having to get off.

One day I went to the market, did some shopping, and was coming back again with a bag hanging on my handlebars. Whoosh down the slope into the ravine.

Too late I saw that there was a pile of broken bricks lying under the water in the middle of the ford, where they'd obviously bounced out of the back of a truck.

I managed to keep the shopping out of the water. I probably shouldn't have tried. My elbow connected with the bricks.

I cycled the rest of the way back to Bartola pouring blood, and was patched up with turmeric paste (natural antiseptic) and a large leaf for a bandage. It was clearly a good job – I don't think the scar would have been any less with modern medical treatment, in fact I'd probably have contracted MRSA in the casualty department. I've still got the scar.

My sturdy Indian bike was unhurt.

Greg and I used to cycle a lot. We tried a tandem, and as a means of getting from A to B it was fine – with me on the back.

It took a bit of getting used to. Ideally, the person on the back should be like luggage with legs – legs to help push the pedals, but luggage that doesn't try to steer, and doesn't resist the leaning of the bike in whatever way the person on the front wants to lean it. This is apparently easy enough for someone who's never ridden a solo bicycle, but it's quite a challenge for a cyclist, initially at least. But Greg weighed two and half times what I did, and didn't notice me straining at the rear handlebars. Eventually I learnt to be luggage with legs, which made things much easier for me but made no noticeable difference to him.

We tried with Greg on the back, but it was impossible for me. It would probably have been very difficult anyway. Thirteen stone of luggage would have been hard to handle – I weighed under six stone myself. But Greg wasn't luggage with legs, and we couldn't stay aboard long enough for him to learn to be. We gave up after the fourth attempt. We'd not managed to get a hundred yards without falling off.

But on the back, I couldn't see much at all. This didn't matter just going from A to B, but for holiday touring it was no good. Thankfully we realized that before we went on cycling tours on the continent, which we did during two of my summer holidays. We took two solo machines.

That had its own problems. I'm a pretty confident and fit cyclist, but I'm a small woman and Greg was a large and equally fit man. He could average sixteen miles an hour all day; I could only manage about thirteen. I struggled to keep up with him, and he struggled to stay back with me.

Until we came to the hills. On hills, I left him in the dust. That might seem a little strange, but we worked out why it was: on the flat, it's the ratio of power to wind resistance that matters; on hills, its the ratio of power to weight. My power to weight ratio was better, but my power to wind resistance ratio was worse.

We experimented with him taking all the luggage most of the time, and me taking it all on the hills. It was more trouble than it was worth swapping everything about all the time, and anyway he still left me behind on the flat. It did even us up on the hills, but more by slowing me down than by speeding him up.

Be all that as it may, those were wonderful holidays, and we enjoyed them immensely. For some reason, I remember especially the exhilaration of arriving at the top of the Col de l'Iseran, after the climb up from Bonneval-sur-Arc. I'd had a cup of tea and was boiling the kettle a second time by the time Greg arrived, which made a change – it was usually the other way around.

Incidentally, making tea at the top of the Col de l'Iseran doesn't work very well. Water boils at 91°C at that altitude, which isn't really hot enough. Not too bad if you put the tea leaves in the kettle, though, rather than pouring the water out of the kettle onto them.

Cycling up to that altitude, puffing and panting with exertion, one's breathing adjusts naturally as one climbs. Neither Greg nor I noticed the thinness of the air at all (73% of the density at sea level). People coming up in their cars did – they got out, started to walk around, felt giddy and went and sat down. There were plenty of benches there for them. Funny, really. I suspect that some of them didn't know why they were feeling like that.

MARCH 1993

With a longer holiday than I usually had, I wanted to take a bit of a look around India, rather than simply hotfooting it to Evansganj, staying there for a while, and hotfooting it back to Delhi.

Shanti and Peter's daughter Rosy had just turned ten, and so had Ravi and Sushila's son John – Little John, everyone called him, to distinguish him from his grandfather. It seemed to me that these two oldest children were ready for a bit of an adventure, and I asked their parents whether I could offer to take them on a trip, first to visit Delhi, and then maybe Agra – to see the Taj Mahal – and Jaipur, in Rajasthan. It meant taking them out of school, but I thought that the adventure would be at least as good an education as they were likely to get at school.

Great excitement. Everyone thought I was right about the educational value of an adventure. The children were delighted at the idea.

On the train to Delhi, we got into conversation with a young Indian man. It's a long journey, and we must have heard practically his whole life story.

His name was Sulwesi Adams. I should tell you how to say that: Sull (like pull) – way – ssy (like fussy).

If you think it's a funny name, you're not alone – it's a funny name to an Indian ear, too. His mother died when he was born, and his father left him and his big sister with the local missionary's wife, Mrs Adams. His father left the village, and they've never seen or heard of him since.

Sulwesi's sister has got a sensible name, Prema, because she had it already. But Mrs Adams gave Sulwesi his name. She could have asked his auntie to give him a proper name, or she could have given him an

English name; but no, she would make up what she thought was a nice Indian sounding name.

If it was Indian at all, it would probably be a girl's name. It would be quite a nice name for a girl.

There's an island in Indonesia called Sulawesi. Maybe that's where Mrs Adams got the name, maybe subconsciously. The island used to be called Celebes – at least by Western atlas publishers. Celebes – Sulawesi. Different attempts by Angrezi to pronounce the same word? At least his name is pronounceable, by Indians or by Angrezi.

Mrs Adams could have asked their auntie to look after them too, and they'd have grown up like their cousins. But their father apparently wasn't on speaking terms with their mother's family, and he'd asked Mrs Adams to look after them, so she did. No real thought for them – her first concern was about the promise she'd made to their father. Perhaps she thought he'd check up on her, or perhaps she thought that God was watching her carefully and was more concerned with the letter of her promise than the spirit of thoughtfulness and kindness to the children.

She had no real thought for them – in one sense. In another sense, she couldn't have been kinder. When they were little, they really were treated as part of the family. Sulwesi shared a room with David, and Prema shared a room with Susan. They were just like brothers and sisters.

Then they all went to school together in the little school in the church in the village. The teacher, Pastor Samson, tried his best to treat them all the same. None of them realized until much later that it was more than he could manage to treat the Adams children the same as he treated all the other children from the village. It was just the way things were. In Pastor Samson's mind, Prema and Sulwesi came somewhere in between the English children and the Indians. At that stage of their lives they were closer to David and Susan than they were to the other Indian children.

At home, Dr Adams gave the four of them extra lessons. All four did exactly the same stuff. They learnt all kinds of geography and English history and grammar that no one else in the village was doing. Their spelling and the breadth of their vocabulary mattered; and of course the conversation in the home was quite different from everyone else's, but they didn't realize that until years later. At school they were the four star pupils, but there was never any sign of ill feeling. It was just the way things were. Pastor Samson, himself Indian but raised in a missionary household, taught everything in English, with Hindi just another subject. Their first language was English, but for the other children it was an extra hurdle.

A lady, Muni her name was, used to come up from the village to cook and clean for the Adamses, and sometimes look after the children if Mrs Adams was out or busy. The four children learnt Hindi from Muni when they were little, and looking back Sulwesi thinks she knew it was going to be more important for him and Prema than for the other two, or perhaps she just loved them a little more. Sulwesi and Prema certainly got better at Hindi than Susan and David did. But Muni was illiterate, and it was Dr Adams who taught them Hindi writing and grammar, long before Pastor Samson started on it at school. David and Susan were just as good at written Hindi as Prema and Sulwesi were, but in speech they always sounded like English kids talking Hindi, and Sulwesi thinks he and Prema never did.

The first time Sulwesi and Prema realized that they were not really part of the family was when they all went to Mussoorie to look at the boarding school. David and Susan were going to go there – and Sulwesi and Prema weren't. You couldn't really blame the Adamses: the Mission Society was paying the fees, and the Mission Society didn't accept Sulwesi and Prema as their children. The fees were too much for the Adamses to pay out of their own pocket – they wouldn't have sent David and Susan if the Mission Society hadn't been paying. And why should the local church spend a large part of its meagre income sending Sulwesi and Prema to boarding school? Why them rather than any of the other Indian kids?

The final blow came when the Adamses had to go back to England. Mr Adams was too sick to stay in India. The Indian immigration rules had changed, and there wasn't going to be another English missionary to replace him. The Indian staff were going to have to carry on the work without support from England – not even any money.

Sulwesi and Prema had never been properly adopted. I don't know if it would have been any different if they had been adopted. They were Indian citizens, and there was no way they were going to be allowed to go to England.

Perhaps they'd have been misfits in England. They didn't feel much different from David and Susan, but by then those two had had four years in a posh boarding school, while Sulwesi and Prema had carried on in the local school system. They certainly felt like misfits among their Indian peers, but they were probably more Indian than English by then. After David and Susan went to boarding school they were left much more to their own devices, and got to know their real relatives properly for the first time.

It was only after the Adamses left that Sulwesi and Prema discovered that the Adamses had been paying fees for them at the local school. All the other kids who passed their exams were getting their fees paid by the Government under a tribal support scheme; but they weren't tribal – not so far as the authorities were concerned. Their parents were English and therefore not tribal; more to the point, they were regarded as rich kids. When the Adamses left they felt like orphans. Who was going to pay their fees now?

Auntie sorted that one out. She just filled the forms in for them as Prema and Suleman, with her own surname instead of Adams, and that was that. Their headmaster knew, but he also knew why. After that, everyone called Sulwesi Suleman for years, which he was quite happy about because it saved a lot of explaining, but he still felt like Sulwesi inside.

They'd had a good start in their education, of course, so they did well. They passed all their exams and got every scholarship that was going, and they've both ended up in good posts. Sulwesi's in Delhi now and Prema's in Bhopal, and they see each other whenever they can, and write to each other a lot. They keep hoping Prema will be able to get a transfer to Delhi but there never seems to be a chance. Both of them miss their Auntie and their cousins a great deal. They only manage to see them once a year.

For a long time they missed the Adamses too. David and Susan had promised they'd write to them, but they never did, and Prema and Sulwesi didn't even have their address. Dr Adams sent them Christmas cards for years, but he never thought of giving them his address. The first few times he wrote a few lines of family news, but then it was just a card, and then it stopped coming altogether – or maybe Auntie started hiding them and pretending they hadn't come, because she knew how much they always upset Sulwesi and Prema.

Sulwesi wondered what would happen if he was too sick to stay in India, or Prema was. It was a purely rhetorical question, of course: what happens to anyone who's too sick for the available health service to cope with?

I promised to try to trace the Adamses for Sulwesi. He probably thought that nothing would come of it, but I'm not like that. I did manage to trace them.

When I found them, I wasn't sure whether to tell him their news, but decided that however badly it might affect him and his sister, I'd better keep to my word. I didn't know whether that was the right decision, but it's what I did.

The easiest way to tell the story is to copy part of my letter to him:

> The Adamses were in a car crash five years ago, and David was killed. Dr Adams has been in a wheelchair ever since, but Susan and Mrs Adams weren't seriously hurt. Dr Adams has kept on sending you Christmas cards, so presumably Auntie has been hiding them. He is old and frail now. His mind is still sharp, but Mrs Adams isn't all there at all. How they manage at all is a miracle: he's her brains, and she's his feet.
>
> Dr Adams never managed to get a job after they came back to England, so they've not been well off at all. Mrs Adams did a cleaning job for a few years, and then she worked as a school dinner lady until she got too confused to cope. David started at University but dropped out. He did a couple of dead-end jobs, then he was training as an electrician until he was killed. Susan went to University and got a degree, and now she's married and has two small children.
>
> Dr Adams was very pleased to hear how well you two are doing. I gave him your address in Delhi so that he could avoid the Auntie trap, but he was very unsure about whether it would be a good thing to write to you, after so long, or not. Like I say, he was very pleased to hear how you were doing, but he'd made a decision when they left that it would be fairer to you two not to let you have their address, and force you to find your own way. He knew you'd have to anyway, and he thought it would be better for you not to have an illusory lifeline.
>
> I don't know how to put this, but he still seems to think the same way a bit. He asked me not to give you his address, and let him make his own mind up.
>
> It seems to me that you have more to offer him than vice versa these days, but that's really equally illusory. He can no more go to live in India again than you could have come to England, and even though you're well off in India, you can't send him money. Even if you could, a lot of rupees doesn't come to many pounds and would go nowhere in England at English prices.

I gave Sulwesi my own address. It was a while before he replied. Amongst other things he wrote was this:

> Auntie was funny. After all those years of pretending not to have had any post from the Adamses, and without me saying anything, she told

> us this year that Dr Adams hadn't sent a card – and went and got the old ones. She'd kept them all. She thought that perhaps Dr Adams had died, and I told her about you, and all the news. She cried when she heard about David and Dr Adams.
>
> What upset her most, though, was the fact that in England, Dr and Mrs Adams are obviously nobody special at all.

We've been corresponding ever since, and we've met in Delhi again a couple of times. A quite charming young man, now with an equally charming young wife.

Dr Adams died a couple of years later, and Mrs Adams went to live with Susan and her family. Susan found my address in Dr Adams's papers and wrote to me to let me know. I gave Susan Sulwesi's address and she wrote to Sulwesi too, and asked him to tell Prema – as if she needed to tell him! Sulwesi told me that it was strange to read Susan's letter, and it made him feel very peculiar. He said that her handwriting was just the same as it used to be, but he could tell that her way of thinking had changed completely. At long last, she sent him her address.

Nowadays apparently the Christmas cards go both ways, with little bits of news. Sulwesi wonders if he and Prema will ever see Susan again – to quote one of his letters to me, "Changed though she is, she seems a very nice person."

I've never met Susan myself – I met Dr and Mrs Adams just once.

March 1993

Back to that train trip when I first met Sulwesi, when I was taking Rosy and Little John for their big adventure.

We told Sulwesi about our planned adventure, and he discouraged us from going to Agra.

"It's horrible. Agra attracts India's rip-off artists like wasps to a picnic. It's bad enough for an Indian, unless they look like a beggar – but for Angrezi? Horrible. It would be especially horrible for you, Penny, because all the rip-off artists will see you as just another Angrezi woman, without even a man to protect you."

"Worse than Connaught Place?"

Connaught Place is the centre – conceptually though not geographically – of New Delhi. It's a magnet for tourists, for Indians from other parts of India as much as for foreigners. Sulwesi's description would almost have fitted Connaught Place – a bit of an exaggeration, but with a certain amount of truth to it.

"Oh, Connaught Place is all right. No, Agra is a thousand times worse. You can't trust the taxis or autorickshaws to take you where you want to go. The only way to visit Agra safely is on an organized tour, and then you'll spend more time in malodorous souvenir shops than at the Taj Mahal or any other site you actually want to see."

What he said rang true, and we decided to change our plan. Rosy and Little John were very pleased to be involved in discussion about it. With Sulwesi's encouragement, we eventually decided that we'd try to visit Mussoorie.

"It's a lovely place. Prema and I were so jealous of David and Susan going there, but it's probably just as well that we didn't. We'd have been in real trouble when the Adamses left if we had."

Sulwesi wasn't able to give any advice about where to stay when we got to Mussoorie; but our hosts in Delhi gave me a list of guest houses. "It might be pretty cold there though – winter isn't always over yet up there at this time of year!"

The very next morning, long before dawn, we got a taxi to the Interstate Bus Terminus, where we were to catch a bus to Mussoorie. It's possible to go by train as far as Dehradun, but it takes longer and is more expensive. Next time I go to Mussoorie – and there's got to be a next time, it's a lovely place – I might try the train. You'll probably understand why.

Almost all the buses in India, and all but one of the buses we saw in the Interstate Bus Terminus, are pretty much the same shape and size as typical English single decker buses. The seats are smaller, and there are more of them crammed into the available space – except in the tour buses, which give passengers much the same space as you'd get in England.

But our bus, when it arrived, was different. It was little more than half the length of the others. *Ah*, I thought, *a mountain bus, designed for tight bends on narrow roads with precipitous drops over the edge of the road.*

The bus wasn't overcrowded like the buses around Evansganj. We actually got a bank of three narrow seats to ourselves.

We set off. I could sense something about this bus – something about the noise of the engine. It wasn't until we got onto the main road outside the city that I knew what it was. We had an engine like a big truck, and it was well maintained. The bus didn't weigh nearly as much as a big truck – it was a much smaller than average bus. *Ah*, I thought, *a mountain bus, designed for steep hills.*

The road was busy, with a lot of slow traffic in both directions. But our driver was in a hurry, and he had the performance of a sports car at his disposal. The slightest gap in the traffic in the opposite direction, and he was over the other side of the road, hand on horn and foot to the floorboards.

So the chap coming the other way had to slam on his brakes? Not our problem. Oh dear, that chap had to swerve right off the road? He'll be okay, it's good firm ground there and that's a jeep he's driving.

At least this road was two lanes wide.

In the Evansganj area, the main roads are one lane wide, with a sort of hard shoulder of gravel each side in most places. When you meet anything coming the other way, either one of you has to get off the road completely, or each gets halfway off the road. You creep past each other.

This isn't usually too bad, but sometimes the hard shoulder isn't as hard as it might be – especially during the monsoon. It's not that unusual to see a truck or a bus lying on its side, when the ground has given way under it. Serious injuries and even deaths often result.

On the other hand, I've seen a truck (the one in the picture) righted by a large crowd of men with ropes, little the worse for its experience – a couple of broken windows and some minor dents. I didn't see it go over. It was already down by the time I arrived at the scene on my bicycle. On that occasion apparently nobody had been hurt. There had been a lot of people riding on the load and in the cab, but all except the driver had got down before the attempt to pass the other vehicle – they'd anticipated the possibility of a fall!

I didn't get any usable pictures of the righting, because it was dark by that time. They had to top up the engine oil because a lot had leaked out, but then the engine started without trouble, and off they went.

Although I've ridden in buses quite a lot in India, this was by a wide margin the scariest ride. Not only was the bus being driven by a would-be rally driver, the road was neither one thing nor the other: it wasn't a single track road that you have to take slowly, creeping past the occasional vehicle that you meet coming the other way, and nor was it a good road with smooth-flowing traffic. It was fast and bad. We saw the aftermath of more accidents in a few hours on that road than I've seen in the whole of the rest of my life. Literally.

Of course like most roads in India, progress is not helped by the presence of cows, pigs, chickens, children, cyclists carrying impossible loads on their bicycles, potholes and so forth wandering randomly all over the road. Or, looked at another way, all these legitimate road users are not helped by the presence of motorized vehicles driven as fast as they'll go by maniacs. "As fast as they'll go" varies from quite as fast as similar vehicles might go in England, to little more than a crawl – or, not infrequently, *oops, I've stopped right in the middle of the road, I wonder what's gone wrong now?*

Twice, we detoured completely off the road to bypass snarl-ups around recent accidents. What happens in such circumstances in wet weather when the land beside the road is too soft for such detours, I don't know.

In another place, everything in both directions had to go half off the road because there was a lorry right in the centre of the road with its back axle supported on a substantial chunk of rock, with not only a pair of wheels removed from one side, but the entire drum brake assembly in pieces on the road. There was no-one working on it and I assumed they'd hitched a ride to somewhere to obtain some part or other. How long that truck would be there, I'd no idea. It had gone a few days later when we passed on our way back.

I think most if not all the remains of accidents that we saw on the way back were new ones. The older ones seemed all to have been cleared up, so the large number of them reflected the number of incidents over a relatively short period. Ho hum.

I'm not a hundred percent sure of that observation. I wasn't taking careful note of them! Another time maybe I might.

Some people got snacks or even chai when we stopped at bus stands in the various small towns – but generally we didn't stop long enough for me to be bothered.

We did stop once for a reasonable time at a roadside halt in the middle of nowhere, for everyone to stretch their legs and get a drink – chai for the adults, and fruit juice for the children. Some people were getting snacks too, but we didn't fancy anything that was on offer. I did rather wonder whether the bus drivers were being given a kickback to stop at this particular spot, rather than in the bus stands in town, where there were plenty of little stalls – or maybe it was the bus companies themselves who arranged it, to avoid overcrowding in the town bus stands.

As far as Roorkee and a little beyond, it was hot and dusty. John and Rosy were excitedly watching the scenery, and life on and around the road. It was quite unlike the world around Evansganj, which is well up in the hills. We saw large fields of sugar cane growing, which you never see around Evansganj.

Not long after Roorkee, we went through the Siwalik hills – steep, unstable piles of weak conglomerate, quite different from the hills around Evansganj. They look just like great piles of beach cobbles – and of course that's exactly what they originally were, millions of years ago. Very interesting for me, as well as for the children. And we'd left the heat and the dust behind.

The climb up from Dehradun to Mussoorie is something else. It is steep, and goes on and on and on being steep. It winds back and forth, with tight bends at frequent intervals, sometimes where the hillsides are dissected by deep ravines alternating with sharp edged spurs, sometimes where the road doubles back on itself to head in the other direction across the face of the hill.

This is why the Mussoorie bus has twice as big an engine as most buses have, and half the weight. We roared up that hill at twenty odd miles an hour, passing big trucks crawling up in bottom gear as if they were stationary.

Unlike the bus, the trucks aren't specially made for that route, but a truck's bottom gear is low enough to crawl up the steepest hill, very slowly. So slowly that drivers can get out of their cabs, go for a wee, then go and catch up with their truck again without even having to run.

Okay, I'm sure someone else in the cab takes over the steering! Indian trucks usually have quite a crowd in the cab, some just hitching a ride, others there to assist the driver in various ways – such as dealing with bandits on some routes.

We arrived at the bus stand in Mussoorie just after noon. By that time we were all ravenous. There were foodstalls right there by the bus stand, with the food cooking right there in front of our eyes. We had samosas and chai for lunch.

Stalls like that might seem like risky places to eat, but they're not – they're a good deal safer than fancy restaurants where you can't see what they're doing in the kitchen. Those samosas came straight out of very hot fat – we saw them cooking, so we knew. And the chai was boiling when it went into the glasses, quite hot enough to sterilize the glasses as well.

While I'm going on about safe eating, here's the other useful tip: eat things that come in "God's own packaging". Okay, I'm pretty much an atheist, but it's still a good description. Bananas, oranges, and hard boiled eggs are all pretty safe – as long as you make it clear that you want to peel them yourself! And as long as your own hands are clean of course. I don't mind washing my hands in water that's been sterilized with chlorine tablets, but I'd rather not drink the foul stuff. Not that I'm paranoid about dirty hands anyway – as long as you know what kind of dirt they've got on them. Your immune system can handle most things in moderation really. We didn't wash our hands before eating our samosas. They were probably cleaner than any readily available water.

We followed the instructions we'd been given at the Blue Triangle in Delhi. First we went to the most recommended guest house, Edgehill, although it wasn't the nearest to the bus stand. It did have a room for the three of us. If you're ever in Mussoorie, I recommend it. Assuming it's still there and is still a guest house.

It's quite a climb up from the bus stand to Edgehill. At six thousand feet or so, the air is only twenty percent thinner than at sea level, so it shouldn't make a lot of difference, but it seemed to. Or was it that the air was colder than I'd got used to? Whatever the reason, we all got more breathless on the walk than seemed right.

A ten year old boy, his ten year old female cousin, and their parents' female cousin, aged forty-four, all in one room? Not a problem, we're Indian. Okay, so I'm white, but I was dressed like an Indian and talked

Cooking on a large chulha in a roadside café. A good place for safe food – as long as you only have stuff you've seen very hot recently.

like an Indian and those two really are my cousins' children and they were old enough to confirm it themselves. Oh, and my passport, although it's a British one, says *Place of Birth: Evansganj, India.*

We booked in, arranged to have dinner in the guesthouse that evening, left our things in our room, and went and investigated Mussoorie. It was beautifully sunny, but it wasn't warm. In fact, it was downright chilly. I bought us each a warm jacket, and socks and shoes – we'd all been wearing sandals without socks – in the bazaar.

In some ways, much of Mussoorie is like any other small Indian town. In other ways, it's extraordinary. It's the only place I've ever been in India that is quite so precipitous, with many buildings that are several storeys high on one side, and just one storey high on the other. The roads twist and turn to follow the shape of the hills, and most of them are steep. There are no cycle rickshaws, and very few bicycles.

The centre of the town, like other Indian towns, is densely built up. The buildings have narrow frontages onto the road, jammed together in tight higgledy-piggledy terraces broken by the occasional narrow alleyway or tiny side street.

Away from the centre of town, the buildings are mainly detached and rambling, seemingly built as a series of random extensions to the original construction. A large proportion of the roofs of these rambling buildings are corrugated iron, most of them painted – you can see this because you're looking down on the top of the ones on the downhill side of the road.

Between them, the hillsides are clad with mature woodland, mostly pine. Nowhere is flat. Everywhere the ground slopes around forty-five degrees, except immediately each side of each road, where on one side the ground has been cut away for the road, and on the other side it's been built up for the road. We saw several places where part of the road had collapsed down the hill, or where there had been a landslip onto the road, often undermining a tree, leaving its roots exposed.

Up and down, up and down we went exploring. Our bags weren't heavy, but without them we felt much lighter. Nonetheless, in the thin cold air we exhausted ourselves quite quickly, and around sunset we arrived back at Edgehill ready for supper and bed. We were conscious that we hadn't reached the top of any of the hills, and while we'd had spectacular views to the south, over the Doon valley and of Mussoorie itself and the hillsides below it, we hadn't seen to the north, or the high Himalayan mountains.

Apart from us, there were two groups staying at Edgehill: an American family, and a small group of students from Delhi. We all ate supper together.

The Americans weren't actually missionaries as far as I could tell, but they certainly believed in trying to ram their Christianity down everybody's throats.

I've met missionaries in India several times, and they seem to fall into two categories.

There are those who live and work for years in remote villages, running little hospitals and helping people around them, and only mentioning their Christian convictions when asked why on Earth they spend their lives serving others. Their obvious sincerity and dedication cannot fail to impress, and a few of the people who ask them this question are so impressed that they are converted to Christianity. Converts like that stay converted, generally. These missionaries don't make huge numbers of converts, but those they do convert are real converts.

I don't share their beliefs, but I can't help admiring them.

Then there are those who visit India for a few days, weeks or even occasionally months, hold massive rallies and preach to thousands. They often offer little gifties – maybe a sari or a dhoti or a towel – to attendees. They invite people to come forward and declare their conversion, or receive the Holy Spirit, or whatever, and a few prepared supporters come forward to encourage others. They "convert" hundreds to Christianity at their rallies, and then go back to their comfortable guest houses in Delhi or Mumbai – where they boast to each other about how many converts they've made. I've heard them. It's excruciating.

The pain is somewhat eased by the thought of all the recipients of the little gifties saying "thank you very much", and then going home and doing puja. I've met quite a few of them, too, and had a good laugh with them.

And then the pain comes back when you think of the impecunious congregation in some some small American town, scrimping and saving to fund the missionary's trip. Little realizing that what their precious missionary is really doing is having a nice little holiday in India at their expense.

Which is all complicated by the fact that a tiny minority of Hindus have the idea that they should "reconvert" Indian Christians to Hinduism. They typically also hold huge rallies, offer gifties to attendees, and boast to each other about the numbers reconverted. And again, the recipients of the little gifties typically say, "thank you very much", and then go back to their church to pray for forgiveness.

The majority of the people they're trying to convince themselves they're reconverting are either Adivasi or Dalit.

The Adivasis mostly weren't Hindu before they were Christian anyway – except in the sense that Hinduism is quite happy to include any other religion, or even agnosticism and atheism, under its umbrella. They'd be quite happy to add Christ to their pantheon – many of them do. The problem they have with Christianity, and Islam for that matter, is that Christians and Muslims reject all the other Hindu gods.

The Adivasis never minded in the slightest if any god or gods they might or might not have believed in got included in someone else's pantheon, even if only as some sort of second rank deities. They just went on their own sweet way regardless. Whether they even had gods is moot. Christians and Hindus came along and insisted on seeing everybody's cultures in terms of religion, but what the truth is, who knows?

I've heard some Hindus claim the Adivasis were Hindu before the Christian missionaries came; and I've heard Christians – calling themselves "anthropologists" – say "No, no, they were animists." I've talked at length with Adivasis myself, and what they mostly say is, "Oh, we'll tell the nutcases anything to keep them happy" and then we share a good belly laugh.

That's not my Adivasi relatives. Chhoti and her family are all Christian, as are Sushila's, Jyoti's and Peter's – although many of them are culturally Christian but agnostic or atheist in actual belief, like both Uncle John and me. But in Bartola where Sushila comes from only about two thirds of the people are Christian, and in Jyoti's village Navadih only about one third of them are. It's no problem to talk about these things with anyone in either village. Everybody's perfectly friendly. Very often even the Christians have a similar view of things – the Adivasi Christians, that is, and Christians of Dalit origins. Upper caste Christians – which seems to me to be a bit of a contradiction in terms, but its reality on the ground is undeniable – often seem to have a very different view, much more like that of the European, American or Australian anthropologists.

It's scarcely surprising that Adivasis and Dalits feel little attachment to Hinduism, a religion that puts them at the bottom of the pile! That's not to say they don't enjoy the Hindu festivals – but then the less uptight Christians enjoy the Hindu festivals too, and the less uptight Hindus enjoy Christmas as well. They'd all happily celebrate Chinese New Year with the Chinese, given half a chance. Any excuse for a good time – it doesn't mean you have to believe in anything at all.

Of course the *more* uptight Christians frown on their fellow Christians enjoying Holi or Diwali or Dussehra or whatever; and the more uptight Hindus, who are a tiny minority, frown on their fellow Hindus enjoying Christmas day, or even worse, St Valentine's day. Both groups are fighting a losing battle, and thank the deity of your choice for that.

I'll happily join with anyone frowning on celebrating Mammon on any of these occasions. Am I being inconsistent?

I was talking about the dinner that first night at Edgehill, if I remember aright. There was the evangelizing American family – Dad, Mum, small son and daughter – and there was the group of Delhi students. And there was us.

The Americans initially assumed I was another of their kind, and I certainly didn't want to have any arguments with anyone, so I didn't disabuse them. For one thing, I knew that the guest house owners themselves had missionary connections – they were, after all, the establishment that got the highest recommendation from the Blue Triangle in Delhi. And of course Rosy and Little John were being brought up in the Christian community in Evansganj, although I had a suspicion that they were growing up as fairly secular Christians, very possibly agnostic ones. But I hadn't discussed the questions with them, and over dinner in a very Christian guest house didn't seem the right moment to do so.

The Americans equally seemed to assume that the Delhi students were Hindu – not by any means a safe assumption, since they were staying in a distinctly Christian establishment, which the students probably hadn't chosen at random.

The Delhi students were very polite. They were obviously as conscious as I was that they were guests in a Christian establishment, but they did seem to be avoiding rising to any of the American bait. Perhaps they were Hindu after all – they obviously weren't Muslims, and didn't seem to be Sikhs either – or perhaps they just found the Americans a bit embarrassing. After all, I was avoiding rising to any of the bait, either – and my cultural background is Christian.

Eventually the Americans went off, probably to bed. We'd been tired when we first arrived at dinner, but squirm as I might, I couldn't help but be fascinated by the goings-on. As soon as the Americans had gone, one of the students turned to me, and nearly collapsed in giggles.

"Weren't they hilarious!" In English. I had said the odd word in English, so it was a fair guess – although it's a general assumption in India that a white person will speak English. But thank goodness for that reaction, anyway!

"They were. We're from a Christian background, but they were embarrassing."

"We could see you were thinking that. We're a mixed bunch, two Hindus and a Sikh, but the rest of us are Christians. But they had a terrible attitude."

"Well, exactly."

Ice broken, we got chatting about all kinds of things, and ended up staying up late. Once dinner was over, the guest house owners and staff had disappeared, and we all let our hair down rather.

I know not all Americans are like that! They don't even have a monopoly on it, although somehow in India at least, it does seem to be Americans more often than anyone else.

The students mentioned that they'd visited Surkanda Devi the day before, and enthused about it. It's the highest peak in the area, and quite accessible. You can get a bus to a point just over a mile from the summit. It's a steep climb, but a good path. From the top, you get good views of the high Himalayas.

They'd also visited various waterfalls in the area. All in all, they'd enjoyed their visit. They were leaving the following day, which they said was a pity, "We'd have enjoyed having your company!"

I thought that was a very nice thought, especially considering that I was twice their age, and Rosy and Little John half. We said our goodnights on the very best of terms. We had decided to visit Surkanda Devi the following day, and a waterfall or two the day after that.

The following morning, the students left for the Delhi bus straight after breakfast. We bid each other farewell in a very friendly fashion, somewhat to the bewilderment of the Americans, who stood and waved from the verandah as they left.

We went down to the bus stand not long after the students, to catch our bus to Surkanda Devi. The bus actually heads from there past a point much closer to Edgehill, where the bus will stop on request – but we were told at the guest house that if it's already full, it doesn't always stop, so we didn't take any chances.

It wasn't full at all. There were plenty of spare seats.

The sky was grey. We should perhaps have taken more notice. If it was chilly in the sunshine the previous afternoon, it was doubly so under grey skies in the morning. We huddled together in the unheated bus.

It wasn't just unheated. Half the windows were missing, too.

We sped along the narrow, rough road, with sharp bends left and right, in and out of the gulleys down the steep wooded slopes. We were probably never doing much over thirty miles an hour, often less, but it seemed like breakneck speed on that road. In places, the surface was just loose stones or mud, and most of the way there was barely room for two vehicles to pass. In some places, it wasn't even that wide. On our left, it was often almost vertically upwards, and on our right, almost vertically downwards for the first dozen feet, and then forty-five degrees or steeper after that. At least there were plenty of trees to break our fall should we have left the road.

Reassuringly, there was no sign of crashed vehicles amongst the trees, or even of damaged trees where a vehicle had crashed but been recovered. Somehow I couldn't imagine anyone attempting to recover a vehicle anyway. Strip it for parts, certainly, but recover it? Doubtful. The battered body shell would stay there rusting until it rusted away completely. Years and years and years.

Along the road, we saw children waiting for a bus in the other direction, presumably going to school in Mussoorie. That was for the first dozen miles. After that, we started picking children up. They were going to school in Dhanaulti. I know that for sure. They had their school bags with them, and they all got off in Danaulti. They chattered cheerfully, as children do. We couldn't help listening in. Their Hindi wasn't quite the same as either Evansganj or Delhi Hindi, but the difference was slight, more in pronunciation than anything else, so they were perfectly comprehensible. We didn't hear anything very enlightening!

After Dhanaulti, we started seeing children waiting to go the other way again, but from there it's not far to the Surkanda Devi stop.

The bus stop at Surkanda Devi is at a col, with the climb to Surkanda Devi on one side, and a small hill on the other. I don't know what it's like now, years later, but at that time there was a gravelly, muddy parking area beside the road, almost filling the relatively level area in the col, with room for maybe fifteen or twenty cars at a squeeze. Around the edge of the parking area there was a semicircle of little "hotels" – ramshackle shelters with mud floors, a table or two, some benches or chairs, crude cooking facilities, and cheerful proprietors who'd serve you chai and a snack or even a simple meal. All freshly cooked right there in front of your eyes, and undoubtedly absolutely delicious.

That's what hotel has come to mean in much of India. Language changes like that. Our word "camera" comes from Latin camera, a room, and that from Greek κάμαρα (kamara), an arch. Where the obviously related Hindi word कमरा (kamara), also a room, fits in, I don't know; but I have to suspect it's originally from Sanskrit, which would predate the Greek. And I've heard it suggested in India that कंबल (kambal), a blanket, is really the origin of कमरा – via an intermediate meaning as a room within a tent, constructed of blankets in the fashion of a Mongolian yurt. This isn't as far-fetched as it sounds, given the way MB and M, and R and L have a tendency to mutate into each other over time.

For example, Hindi has four consonants in the space where English only has L and R – one of which can confuse the English ear no end until it gets used to it. Is it an L or an R? English people can't tell. I can, of course, having learnt Hindi at my Ayah's knee. Just to confuse still further, it's often written as D in transliteration into English – and the Hindi letter, ड़, is just the same as the Hindi letter ड – one of Hindi's four Ds (all with distinct pronunciation, although again the English ear might have a hard time distinguishing them) – but with a dot underneath.

If you think that with those etymological speculations I'm straying into areas where I'm no scholar, you're right, but I make no apologies for it. Real scholars are usually pretty tentative, especially about anything very far back in the mists of time. Somehow their tentative conclusions have a tendency to become much firmer by the time they arrive in less scholarly publications, often much to the annoyance of the original scholars, if they take any notice at all of the popularizations. The speculations I'm reporting are very tentative, and I'm more than happy to be shot down in flames by anyone who knows, or even who thinks they know, better. But seriously, I doubt if it's possible to know one way or the other.

Sorry, I digressed again. It wasn't long since we'd had breakfast. We thought maybe we'd have time to get lunch here between arriving back from the summit, and the arrival of our bus back to Mussoorie.

The path up to the summit is very easy to follow. It's steep and quite rough, but not difficult at all as long as you're reasonably fit. By the top, you're almost exactly at ten thousand feet above sea level, and the air is noticeably thin – only seventy percent the pressure of air at sea level – or is it just the cold and the exertion that makes one feel a little light headed and breathless?

It was really cold at the top. The wind had been light at the bus stop, but up at the top is was blowing quite hard. The students had seen the high Himalayas from up there the previous day, but the day we were up there, they were shrouded in cloud. We did get a wonderful view of the Himalayan foothills round about us, though, and little villages and terraced fields in the valleys below us.

There's a famous temple at the summit, I know, but somehow it's expunged itself from my memory entirely. I simply don't remember even seeing it, although I must have been aware of it at the time. I have photographs that I took from the summit, but not a sign of the temple in any of them.

No, that's not a prejudice against Hindu temples. I remember plenty of others perfectly clearly, and I've nothing against them at all, any more than I've anything against stupas, mosques, synagogues or churches. Many of them, of whichever religion, are stunning pieces of architecture, and I've taken lots of photographs of them.

It's just a hole in my memory. I reckon my memory's generally pretty good, but now I know it's got holes. Well, one at least.

I do have good reason to suspect that the current temple on the site is a great deal bigger than what was there in 1993, however.

I took a few photographs, but we were all getting very cold, and the cloud base wasn't very far above us – in fact, there were wisps of cloud *below* us in some directions. We decided it was time to set off down again.

It began to snow before we were even half way down. Fortunately it wasn't a real blizzard, and the path and its potholes and pitfalls remained easy to see.

By the time we got back to the bus stop, it was time for lunch. We had plenty of time before the bus back to Mussoorie would arrive, so we ate in one of the hotels. It was good to be down out of the wind, but we were still very cold. And it was still snowing, maybe a little harder.

I asked one of the men in the hotel whether it often snowed as late in the spring as that, and he just gave a noncommital gesture, as if to say,

"Sometimes it snows, sometimes it doesn't, I've never thought about when."

By the time the bus arrived, there was a covering of two or three inches of snow. The bus arrived pretty much on time, though. We didn't seem to go much slower on the way back than we had on the way out, except that the driver had to stop every now and then for one of his colleagues to remove the snow from the windscreen. The windscreen wipers weren't working.

It was the same bus we'd caught in the morning, now on its way back from Tehri. And of course it still had half its windows missing.

The road was even scarier with inches of snow on it, but the driver didn't seem the least concerned. He probably thought it more important to get to Mussoorie before the snow got deep enough to risk us getting stuck somewhere, and he was probably right.

We were very, very cold indeed by the time we got back to Mussoorie. The bus dropped us off at the point on the road nearest to Edgehill, and we climbed the steep path through the woods with our feet feeling like lumps of ice. You can imagine how pleased we were to find a blazing fire in the hearth in the lounge.

During the night it snowed more, and by the morning it was clear that we weren't going to go anywhere that day. The American family had been intending to leave for Delhi, but it was clear there would be no bus down to Dehradun. It took a while for our hosts to persuade them that there was no possible means by which they could make the journey, but eventually they resigned themselves to being stuck in Mussoorie for as long as the snow remained. If it was more than two more days, they'd miss their flight back to the USA. They weren't sure whether their insurance would cover it.

Had they noticed our unresponsiveness to their religious zeal? Maybe they had – in fact, I began to wonder whether maybe our hosts had had a word with them. At any rate, they didn't mention religion again in our presence, and we got on just fine. Various combinations of us played Scrabble all morning, the older amongst us taking turns to play various games with the two little Argents.

In the afternoon the sun came out. Mr Argent, Little John, Rosy and I went out together for a walk, if walk is really the right word. We struggled through the snow for a while. It was over a foot deep almost everywhere, and considerably deeper in some places where it had drifted. We didn't get very far, but the woods were stunningly beautiful in the snow and the sunshine. I explained to Little John and Rosy about making a snowman, which they did, after rolling a couple of huge snow rolls. Then we had a bit of a snowball fight, and all got very cold.

We went back and warmed up again by the fire in the lounge.

The snow lasted three days, then one night it rained and rained and rained. The combination of heavy rain and the consequent thawing of a considerable amount of snow resulted in several impressive landslips, some of which had to be at least partly cleared before some of the roads could be used – including the one down to Dehradun. It was astonishing how quickly that was done. Well, astonishing to me; but apparently routine to the inhabitants of Mussoorie.

The Argents had missed their flight, of course. We exchanged addresses, but I never wrote to them, and they never wrote to me.

We spent three days in Delhi before catching the train back to Evansganj. We visited the Red Fort, Qutab Minar, and the railway museum. We went window shopping in Connaught Place, and actual shopping in Chandni Chowk. But I don't need to tell you about those places, there's a million people can tell you about them.

We never got to see any of the wonderful waterfalls near Mussoorie, and we never saw the high Himalayas. But Little John and Rosy saw *snow* – lots of it – and played in it. They were very impressed, and apparently they've remembered it as a wonderful holiday ever since.

About 1985

Courtney had hit Eileen *again*.

Neither of them was in my class, but the head reckoned I knew them both better than their class teachers did – I taught them both physics – so it fell to me to visit their parents. So that was *that* evening done for. Marking delayed a day yet again. Ho hum.

Big Courtney had hit little Eileen. So Courtney's the bully, and Eileen's the victim? Well – yes and no.

You've heard how psychological bullying can be as bad as, or even sometimes worse than, physical bullying? How true that is.

Eileen was a small girl, not much bigger than me, but was the prime mover in a group of posh girls who teased Courtney mercilessly about her accent and grammar.

Courtney was a big, clumsy girl. She had no friends in the top sets, although she was in top set for everything except English, and near the top of the class in most of the unsetted subjects. She didn't have many friends in the school at all.

Most of the posh parents wanted Courtney expelled from the school, and kept saying we were being soft on bullying.

What can you do?

Courtney hadn't hit her very hard really. She'd reached the end of her tether and lashed out, but even then, she'd taken care not to hit too hard. If she'd just whacked her as hard as she could, Eileen would have been a hospital case – possibly worse, if she'd landed badly.

They were thirteen or fourteen at the time.

Courtney left school at sixteen, and the last time I saw her she was working as an assembler in an electronics factory. She said she wasn't very good at it – too fiddly for her big hands and poor co-ordination. A great shame – she was a very clever girl, much cleverer than Eileen and her middle-class pals. She'd have been perfectly capable of doing Maths or Physics at a good university, and probably gone on to a research career. She got first rate O levels, despite her disadvantaged background.

The last time I saw Eileen, she was a trainee store manager in a retail chain. I don't think that was an appropriate job, either. I can't imagine her being very good with her staff, and probably not with the customers, either.

July 2001

Bob – not the personnel manager from Pericor! A different Bob, of course – was the new bloke in my life. He was a few years older than me, and had retired young quite recently. He'd been living with me for a couple of weeks, and I decided it was time to introduce him to my work colleagues – some of whom had been my friends since our university days decades earlier. Bob met up with us for lunch at the pub on Friday, and we all had quite a boisterous session, laughing and joking and playing pool.

Then Bob went off and we all went back to work. I didn't have a good afternoon – I couldn't concentrate, and developed a bit of a headache. In fact, I felt a bit ill. About three o'clock, I decided it was time to call it a day. I told Bill, at the desk next to mine, that I was going to go home because I wasn't feeling very well, and got up – and felt really giddy and nauseous. Apparently I went white and tottered a bit.

"You really aren't well, Penny. You can't cycle home in that state. I'll drive you home."

Then I really did totter, and Bill caught me. He got a whiff of my breath.

"Your breath smells of alcohol, Penny!"

I'm tee-total, and the whole office – and Bob – knew that.

"Sit down, Penny. I'm going to ring the pub. What were you drinking?"

I'd never tried pineapple and grapefruit juice mix before. Bob had suggested it. Perhaps it's better without the vodka. The barman confirmed Bill's suspicions, and apologized for not realizing someone was playing evil games. I'd always trusted my colleagues, and I'm sure that trust was warranted. I'd thought I could trust Bob, too. Ho hum.

I got my key back from Bob that evening, and a grovelling apology. And threw him out, bag and baggage. I didn't know where he went that evening, and I didn't care. I hoped I'd never see him again. Had he thought about the fact I still had an afternoon's work to do? That I would be cycling home across the city in a couple of hours? That two vodkas is actually quite a lot for someone of such small bodyweight, especially one not accustomed to alcohol?

The following day, I changed the locks. It probably wasn't necessary, but it doesn't cost a lot if you do it yourself. It was annoying, not having my bike for the weekend, but it wasn't worth going into work to get it. I got the bus into work on Monday.

October 2003

The train stops for ten minutes at Kanpur Central. I got out to stretch my legs, look at the magazine stall, and get something to eat.

I bought some sabji in a leaf-bowl, and some puri in another. Then I bought a couple of magazines – the English and Hindi editions of the same issue of India Today, to compare the content and to see how close the translations were of any articles that were in both versions. I got into conversation with the magazine vendor. I wasn't worried about the possibility that the train might set off – I knew that the train would set off gently, and I'd have plenty of time to run and get onto it while it was still moving slowly enough to get on easily.

The train began to move as I was paying, and I was quite a long way behind my carriage – but I didn't worry, I was nimble and knew how gently the train accelerated. I got my change and set off up the platform to catch up with my own carriage. I wanted to get into my own coach, because the corridor connection isn't continuous – there's no connection between the unreserved and reserved sections. I didn't want to have to clamber around the outside of a moving train. I'd done it a few times, but it wasn't my favourite activity by any means.

So there I was, running alongside the train, just getting to my own coach, when bang, one of those long two-wheeled baggage wagons swung sideways into me, bashing against me, just as I was right alongside the gap between two coaches. Over I went, down between the carriages, banging my head first on the buffers and then on the edge of the platform as I slipped between them. I felt my arm and maybe a rib or two break as the corner of the carriage banged into me. My leg buckled awkwardly under me. I thought I was a goner, but there was enough space between the rails and the platform, and I didn't end up under the wheels. One of my plaits fell across the rail and was chopped short as a wheel rolled over it, but that was all.

I lay there hoping nothing sticking out of the underneath of the side of any of the carriages would hit me.

Then I heard a huge voice booming out, "Chain pull! Train rookhiye! Larki train ke niche gir gayi hai! Kooli! Dauro, dauro, chalati ko bolo gari rookhiye, larki gari ke niche hai!" – Pull the communication cord! Stop the train! There's a girl fallen under the train! Coolie! Run, run, tell the driver to stop the train, there's a girl under it!

There were lots of running footsteps. I don't know whether it was the chain or the coolie that got through to the driver, but after what seemed an age the brakes came on with a great squealing, and the train stopped.

Right in front of me a wide pipe hung down just above the rail, dripping – the toilet outlet. On the sleeper, next to the rail and just in front of my face, I could see human shit. My head hurt – I hurt all over. I knew my left arm was broken, and probably my right leg and a rib or two. But I was alive and conscious, and the train had stopped.

A large Sikh gentleman in a respectable suit appeared just the other side of the rail from me. He'd evidently crawled under the carriage. "You're alive! You speak English?"

"Ji han, aur Hindi." Which means, "Yes (respectfully), and Hindi," and our conversation continued in Hindi, but I'll translate.

"Yes, and Hindi. I think I've got a broken leg and a broken arm though."

"Don't worry. I'm a doctor. We'll get you out and get you to the hospital. Where's your leg broken? Thigh or lower leg?"

"Lower leg."

"Thank goodness for that. I'll get some boys with a stretcher. Don't worry. I'll be back in a few minutes."

He was as good as his word. The stretcher turned out to be a sheet of corrugated iron from a building site near the station, but better that than an hour's wait for a proper stretcher from the hospital. They uncoupled the train just ahead of where I was lying, and pulled the rear half of the train back a few yards so they could get me out.

Doctor Singh even made sure someone found all my possessions off the train before he allowed the train to leave.

For some reason, an image of the shit right in front of my face stuck in my mind. It had been very dark green, almost black, with a network of stringy white slime all over it. I wondered if that was symptomatic of some particular disease, but didn't have the courage to ask Dr Singh about it.

I was in Doctor Singh's hospital for two weeks. Ben came out to India to make sure I was being properly looked after, and thinking possibly to arrange my repatriation; but Doctor Singh and I had already decided I'd be better off staying where I was. I was looked after very well indeed.

Hmm. Would taking me to Scotland be repatriation? I'm a British citizen, but I was born in India.

Ben came out again when I was discharged, bringing an electric wheelchair for me. Getting about on crutches had proved to be very difficult with one arm out of action. With an arm in plaster as well as a leg, I couldn't have used an ordinary non-powered wheelchair. You do see one-armed people in wheelchairs in India, with a hand operated crank to drive themselves slowly along. It's amazing how they manage. But their chairs are tailor made for them, because they need them for life. I only needed mine for a few weeks.

Ben accompanied me all the way to Evansganj. I couldn't have got on and off the train on my own.

It was lovely to be in Evansganj, but of course frustrating to be stuck in a wheelchair and very dependent on help from the family. The footpaths, roads and pavements in Evansganj aren't designed with wheelchair users in mind at all. Nevertheless, with a little help from various members of the family – Ravi, Kamal and Shanti's children were mostly in their teens and very helpful – I got around the town.

This is maybe the point to digress a little to remark upon a recurring dilemma. Getting around town when I'm in Evansganj, which is normally easy enough, is partly a matter of revisiting old haunts, seeing how things have changed, and being nostalgic about how things used to be, or in some cases how they still are. It's partly about meeting friends, now I've made friends in Evansganj again. But another part of it is shopping.

I buy most of my clothes in Evansganj nowadays. I'm only there once every couple of years or so, but that's not a problem. I'm not one of those people who feel the need for a vast wardrobe with a complete clear out every few months. I don't even use the whole of my luggage allowance on the plane, and I still scarcely buy any clothes apart from socks and underwear in Britain. Clothes, whether off the peg or made to fit, are much cheaper in Evansganj than anywhere in Britain, and I can get exactly what I want. Since I don't generally want to wear little girl clothes, most of mine have to be made to fit. I may not turn up very frequently, but I'm a very good customer and the tailors know me well. I think we have a good relationship.

That's all well and good, but of course everyone knows I've got Angrezi money, which in Indian terms means lots of money. Evansganj isn't on the tourist trail at all, so the traders have never acquired the habit of ripping off tourists; that's not the problem. Anyway, they know I'm no tyro. I get charged the same price as everyone else.

How much the tendency of traders on the tourist trail to rip off tourists is a matter of ordinary traders acquiring the habit, and how much it's a matter of the tourist trail attracting the kind of traders who are that way inclined anyway, who knows? It could even be that they simply outcompete the more straightforward folks.

But back to my dilemma, which is this: how much should I spoil my cousin's children? And now it's beginning to be their grandchildren, too. They all know I've got lots of money, by their standards if not by British standards. If I don't spoil them enough, I'm being mean; if I spoil them too much, well, they'll be spoilt. I'm not sure there is a happy medium between these two errors, in fact I think they inevitably overlap. I'm a bit mean and I spoil them, too. Ho hum.

I don't have this problem in Britain. I am by a significant margin the wealthiest in the family – for years, I had the best job in the family, and I've no dependants – but the difference isn't more than is common in British families.

Shanti and Peter had just become grandparents for the first time. Their elder daughter Rosy had a little boy, Sunil. He slept very happily on my lap in the wheelchair, with a shawl tied around us both to make sure he didn't fall off when I used my free hand to operate the joystick. Rosy scarcely let Sunil out of her sight, so he didn't come with me on my expeditions, apart from one time I went shopping with Rosy.

Kamal came to Delhi with me. We stayed for a couple of days in Delhi, then he took me to the airport where the airport staff took charge of me. I've never got through an airport so smoothly in my life!

Back in Edinburgh, I was able to get about without anyone accompanying me. I could negotiate most places on my own, and could rely on finding someone to help me in the few situations where I couldn't, such as getting on and off buses. But I was out of my plasters just a couple of weeks after getting back to Edinburgh anyway.

I was surprised at how unsteady I felt when the plasters first came off. The first time I went upstairs was actually quite unnerving – well, not so much the going up, as the coming down again. Fortunately, the handrail is on the right side coming downstairs, and it was my left arm that had been broken. I think I might have shuffled down the stairs on my bottom if it had been the other way round.

On the way back to Delhi going home, Kamal and I got into conversation with a new graduate, a food technologist from Bombay – a very interesting and bright young man. We talked about all sorts of things, and we've stayed in touch ever since. I was right in my assessment of him as bright: he was already assistant Vice President of a major commodity exchange in India just six years later.

I honestly don't remember exactly what we talked about on the train on that occasion, it's all muddled up in my mind with things we've talked about since, or even conversations with other people. One particular conversation does stick in my mind though.

Sid (Siddharth) said, "An ordinary person like an autowallah, a dhobi or the like wears a wrist watch in Mumbai, whereas in Delhi I don't see many wrist watches, not even on wealthy people. This cultural difference could be a reason for the difference in punctuality levels in the two cities."

"That's an interesting observation – but which culture do you prefer?"

"Most definitely Mumbai's."

"Interesting. In cities, I think I agree with you, but I very much like the lack of consciousness of time in the countryside."

"I feel the same. In countryside I'm in the same 'time zone' as everyone else. It peeves me to find that nobody turns up until seven for a six thirty meeting in Delhi, while in Mumbai we can start by six forty-five. My impression is that in Delhi people take it as a measure of their own importance how late they can come and find others waiting for them."

I laughed. "I like that. What's more, despite not wearing a wrist watch, they must have a timepiece secreted about their person somewhere to calculate their lateness carefully."

"I guess there are two considerations. One is the self-importance thing. Political leaders or film stars arriving hours late is not unusual. The other is the expectation that even if they arrive on time, the meeting won't start on time, because everyone else will be late. As a result, hardly anyone is on time. If you tell someone 'the meeting starts at six thirty', they mentally translate it to seven o'clock. Sometimes they even think it aloud."

Sid also has a blog, and one thing he wrote in it I've quoted in full, with his permission, in APPENDIX II, because it's so precisely how I feel about the issue, and so very well put.

I've twice been accused of being involved in a road traffic accident, and failing to stop afterwards. Fortunately on each occasion I had absolutely cast iron alibis – not for myself, but for the vehicle allegedly involved. In both cases the vehicle was off the road at the time the accident was alleged to have occurred, and not in my possession at all. In one case it was in the possession of professional repairers, and in the other case it was in pieces in the University car park, where University security personnel were only too well aware of its presence.

Who would accuse an innocent person of such a crime? Once might be a mistake – although to get the registration matching the make, model and colour of the vehicle (in the first case a bright yellow Land Rover) would be unlikely in that case. Twice?

I don't know anything about the person who accused me the first time. Maybe I should have made more efforts to find out – made more of a fuss at the police station, tried to get them to investigate whether it was really a mistake, or something malicious aimed at me personally. It never occurred to me to push the matter once the police had accepted that I really hadn't been involved in any accident.

The second time, I did find out who'd accused me. Surprise, surprise, he was a known National Front supporter. Whether he was actually a member, I don't know. And of course I was an outspoken opponent of the National Front.

I'm jolly glad that I *did* have a cast iron alibi. At that time, the local police force themselves weren't exactly friendly towards opponents of the NF. (Whether they are now, I simply don't know.) Trying to get the police to prosecute the miscreant for making malicious false accusations was a non-starter.

In over forty years of driving, I've never been involved in a road traffic accident while I was moving. I've managed to avoid quite a few, mostly by swerving or braking hard or both, but on a couple of occasions by driving my Land Rover off the road to get out of the way – never by "accelerating out of danger"! People have run into the back of my car three times while I've been stationary, however. It's harder to get out of the way when you're stationary, especially when there's something right in front of you.

SEPTEMBER 1971.

The first time, there'd been an accident. Two lorries had sideswiped each other on a narrow road somewhere near Abergavenny. The police were already there, controlling the traffic, letting a single lane through, first in one direction, then in the other. I stopped at the tail end of the queue. I'd been stopped long enough to have turned the engine off by the time the next vehicle arrived behind me, but he'd come sailing round the bend too fast, and didn't manage to stop before hitting me. He punted me into the back of the car in front of me. Fortunately I had a policeman as witness to the fact that I'd not hit the vehicle in front until I was pushed, so all the costs were paid by his insurance, and I didn't lose my no claims bonus.

Well, I say "all the costs," but that's not really true. The write-off value of my ancient Morris Minor Traveller was less than the cost of repairs would have been, so all I got was the write-off value. The car was still road-worthy, so I continued to use it for another few months. I had to replace the radiator with one from a breaker's yard, and I had to chain the back doors shut, because the locks no longer held. Overall, I was pretty annoyed, and I reckon I was out of pocket really.

December 1973

The next vehicle I had was a Bedford Crewbus. That was also finished off by someone driving into the back of it, but I was asleep in bed at home at the time. It was parked round the corner from the house, on the hill. I used to park it there so I could bump start it down the hill. It didn't seem worth getting a new battery for an ancient wreck that I was planning to scrap when its tax ran out in a few weeks' time.

As I say, I was asleep in bed. I dreamt that someone was banging the dustbins outside the back door.

The house I was living in was a shared one. There were ten of us living there at the time, if I remember correctly. Some of my housemates burst into my room and woke me up, shouting, "Someone's crashed into your van!"

I got dressed quickly and rushed out. My friends were already there. One of them had rung the police. The driver of the car that had run into my van had somehow managed to get out of his car and was ranting and raving and seemed ready to beat someone up, or try to. He was extremely drunk.

His car was a mess, with the engine pushed back into the middle of the front seat. It's a wonder he wasn't badly hurt, and that he'd managed to get out. The police station wasn't far away, and the police were on the scene pretty quickly.

It was all a bit of a laugh, really. He tried to tell the police that my van had pulled out of a side road right in front of him, but there isn't a side road there. There is an entrance to a school, but it has big gates right by the roadside, and they were locked. My van was rather foreshortened, the doors were jammed firmly shut, there was no-one inside, and the engine was stone cold. Hmmm. Driven out of a non-existent side road? The policeman wasn't convinced.

Luckily he was insured. His insurance paid me the write-off value for the van, no arguments. I wasn't complaining – I'd been going to scrap it very soon anyway. What you lose on the swings, you gain on the roundabouts. Well, I did that time, anyway. My Dad used to say that the only way to make money out of an insurance company was to be a shareholder, and I reckon that's mostly right.

The final laugh was what we found in the road in front of the van: a dried-up chappati, covered in purple paint on one side. Most of us were very puzzled, but Alf enlightened us. Months earlier, we'd all been out for a curry, and he'd taken a left-over chappati and slapped it on the roof of the van, where it had stuck unnoticed until the crash. It had stuck to the paintwork better than the paint had stuck to the van.

There were a couple of other stories concerning that Crewbus.

DECEMBER 1972

The first was moving a friend, Carolyn, from Merthyr Tydfil to Yorkshire. All her stuff pretty much filled the Crewbus. Weight-wise, it was probably a bit overloaded, but I'd got no means of telling.

Only a few miles after we set off, on a blind bend just after Storey Arms at the summit of the A470 in the Brecon Beacons, there was a dreadful noise from the back axle and we ground to a halt. I investigated, and discovered that a rear wheel bearing had failed completely, and the weight of that corner of the vehicle was pressing the brake shoes firmly onto the brake drum.

I always had all my tools with me. We had to unload a bit to get at them, but such is life. I stuck some rocks in front of the other three wheels, jacked up the corner of the vehicle, stuck some rocks under the axle and lowered the weight back onto the rocks. I took off the wheel. I removed the bolts and pulled the halfshaft out, complete with the dead bearing.

I hitch-hiked into Brecon, which was nearer, carrying the half-shaft, but I couldn't find anywhere that had the right bearing. Ho hum. I hitch-hiked back to Merthyr, and managed to get the bearing, but the place that sold it to me couldn't press the old bearing off the shaft, or press the new one on. I found a place that could, and they did.

All this time poor Carolyn was sitting in the van, not having a clue where I'd got to! I didn't want to get my lift to stop for a chat on our way back to Merthyr, but I did get him to hoot. Carolyn heard the hoot, but didn't see me in the car, and at first wondered why he'd hooted. Later on, when I'd been gone such a very long time, she guessed that it might have been me hitching back to Merthyr for some reason.

I hitch-hiked back to the van, reassembled everything, and off we went. All this had cost about six hours. I doubt if the RAC or AA would have attempted a road-side repair. They'd have put the van on a car transporter and taken it to a repair garage, and we wouldn't have got it back for days and days, or depending on our contract, taken us to our destination and then let us sort the repairs out ourselves later. Either way, it would have cost us a lot more delay, and a lot more money, too.

We arrived in Yorkshire very much later than planned, but without further incident.

Are you wondering about a tiny woman, who looked about sixteen, hitch-hiking on her own? I was carrying a large piece of metal, over two feet long with a heavy lump on one end...

But I used to hitch-hike anyway in those days. I suppose I was taking a bit of a risk, but I never worried and never came to any harm. Hell, I crossed roads on my own, too! I probably got lifts more easily than blokes or couples. The villains never got a chance to pick me up, because someone else had already taken pity on me before they turned up.

The nearest I came to any harm hitch-hiking had nothing to do with me being small and female. I got a lift in an Irish lorry. The driver was a lovely man, very friendly and an absolutely perfect gentleman. Not much bothered about the letter of the law though! He was exceeding the speed limit by a considerable margin going up the M6. We were just about to overtake a caravan that was also, I'm pretty sure, exceeding his speed limit by a fair bit and snaking somewhat, when the snaking suddenly became violent, the car driver lost control, the car slid sideways onto the hard shoulder, and the caravan collided with the front of our lorry.

There was a fantastic bang. The windscreen shattered all over us, and there were little bits of caravan all over the road.

Nobody was badly hurt, fortunately.

AUGUST 1973

The other story about the Crewbus was an occasion when I took a crowd of friends out for the day in the Yorkshire Dales. We had a really good day, with a picnic somewhere well up into the Dales. I don't remember exactly where, but maybe somewhere near Muker.

We were on our way back, when a sheep ran out into the road right in front of us. I slammed on the brakes, and almost managed to stop in time, but we'd definitely hit it. It didn't get up and run away, so we got out of the van and looked. It was on its side, trapped under the front bumper, struggling to get free and failing. My friends held onto it and shouted instructions to me as I reversed off it very slowly. It scrambled to its feet and ran off, apparently none the worse for the experience. I hope it didn't curl up and die in a corner later, but I'll never know.

I'm normally quite good at retaining my composure in such circumstances. What happens, happens, it's no use crying over spilt milk. Especially when it wasn't even spilt as far as we knew. But I was really disturbed by it, and felt very weird for several hours afterwards. I managed to drive home okay, but I wasn't at all happy doing it.

It was only several weeks later that a friend, whom I still regard as a friend despite this, although we're rarely in contact nowadays, revealed that the mushroom omelette we'd had on the picnic had been full of little bits of psilocybin mushrooms. It's the only time I've taken non-pharmaceutical drugs, as far as I know. I don't really like taking pharmaceutical drugs, never mind others.

June 1974

The second time someone ran into the back of me while I was actually in the vehicle, I was driving my old Land Rover through the middle of town. There was a queue of people waiting for a bus on my left, close to the edge of the pavement. I was driving quite slowly, as I always do when passing pedestrians close to the road, or anywhere where pedestrians might be close to the road but unseen. As I was passing this queue, a pram suddenly appeared just beyond it, pushed into the road not far in front of me. I slammed on the brakes hard, and stopped with a few inches to spare.

I pulled on the handbrake, and turned the engine off to get out and check that everyone was okay. Just as I was opening the door, therefore at least a couple of seconds after I'd actually stopped, there was an almighty bang and the Land Rover bounced forwards. I leapt out and ran round to the front – where fortunately there was still a gap of a couple of inches between the Land Rover and the pram. The Land Rover hadn't moved much.

Then I ran round to the back, where the car that had hit me – much smaller and lighter than the Land Rover – had itself bounced back and left a gap of a foot or so. I looked at the back of the Land Rover. There was a bit of pale blue paint on the rear chassis member, but there didn't appear to be any damage. I turned to the fellow who was just getting out of his car, and said, "It's all right, mate, you've not done any damage." I may have been a little shaken. I don't think that was necessarily the most appropriate thing to have said anyway, but I hadn't at that point taken in who the chap was, what the car he'd been driving was, or how badly his car was damaged.

At that point, a large hand descended upon my shoulder, and another on the shoulder of the young policeman who'd been driving the police car that had hit me. "Don't worry, kid," a kindly voice said to me, "I saw it all. We'd better go into the station and take statements, but you've nothing to worry about. As long as you've got a driving licence!"

We were right outside the police station. The kindly voice was that of a middle-aged officer who'd been standing on the police station steps.

Several years later, I was in a pub with some friends when a chap walked in whom I thought I recognized, but I couldn't place where I knew him from. He was obviously having the same experience, but at first neither of us said anything. Later on, however, he joined us at the pool table, and we got talking. It turned out that he was the policeman who'd run into the back of my Land Rover. He was very friendly, and told me that he was glad he'd not damaged the Land Rover or pushed me into the pram, and that for him it had turned out to be a good thing. He'd not been happy as a policeman anyway. He'd been moved into a different job in the force where he was even less happy, and had finally left the force and got a different job. I forget now what he said his new job was.

My friends Dilip, Brendan, Kay and Mary went down from Yorkshire to Lowestoft to look at an old boat they were thinking of maybe buying. They went in Brendan's Ford Capri. It was going to be a flying visit, but I couldn't go, because of my work. Dilip left his old MG Midget with me for me to do some repairs.

On the Saturday morning, I was upside-down in Dilip's driving seat, with my head down among the pedals pop-rivetting a new floor panel that I'd made into place, when I heard a voice asking, "Excuse me Madam, are you Miss Lane?"

I extricated myself. It was a policeman. He told me that my friends had had an accident in Norfolk, and that they were all in hospital in Bury St Edmunds.

I completed the repair, telephoned the hospital, and set off in Dilip's car. It was much cheaper to run than my Land Rover, and we all borrowed each other's cars all the time in those days. It was really more like a commune than just a shared house.

Fifty miles down the road the engine faded out. I coasted for a way looking for somewhere to leave the road safely, and pulled off. Bonnet up. No petrol getting to the carb. Plenty in the tank. Petrol in the pipe to the pump – which was a pig to get to, high up in the tunnel over the rear axle. Electricity getting to the pump okay. Knock the pump with a big spanner. Tick, tick, tick! Aha! Stuck pump. I was off again.

Another fifty miles. Same thing again. Ho hum. Straight to the trouble with the big spanner up over the rear axle. Off I go again.

Another forty miles. Not again! Aha! The other side of that tunnel is just behind my back. Will banging my fist on the panel do it? Yes! I didn't even have to stop. I had to do it every forty or fifty miles all the way, but that wasn't difficult and I had no further trouble.

Dilip had been driving, late at night. Brendan was asleep in the front passenger seat, Kay and Mary asleep in the back. Dilip nodded off, and was woken by a blaring horn. They was on the wrong side of the A11, and a heavy lorry was approaching. He swerved violently, and narrowly missed a head-on collision, but couldn't hold the car on the road. They must have been going pretty fast.

At that point the road is on a bit of an embankment. They left the road on the left-hand side, and hit a wooden overhead power line post several feet above the ground, leaving a cylindrical dent a foot deep in the left hand side of the car. Mary was catapulted over Brendan's head, out through the windscreen, and landed in the field. Kay bounced upwards and hit her head on the roof, but remained in the car. Dilip got a dreadful bruise in the shape of the steering wheel, right across his chest; Kay had two dreadful black eyes; the other two had cuts and bruises. Miraculously, that was all.

The car was a write-off. But it was Brendan's car, and he was Irish. The car was registered in Ireland, and had been imported temporarily without paying import duty. It had to go back to Ireland, or Brendan would have had to pay a lot of import duty on it.

Back in Yorkshire, I bought the rear axle of a large van, and a hitch assembly off a caravan, from a vehicle breakers. I made a car trailer, and several of us set off in the Land Rover, towing the trailer, to go and get Brendan's car. We loaded up the car, and set off for Fishguard. Not We'd not got very far when the brakes failed on my home made trailer. I knew they'd failed by the change in the way the Land Rover handled when I braked. I got out and checked, and could see the problem. Unfortunately, it wasn't going to be easy to fix.

At this point, we weren't very far from the village where my old friend Nick had set up a car repair business. I rang him, and arranged with him to fix the brakes for me. We agreed that as long as I drove slowly, it'd be safe enough for me to drive to his garage. It wasn't the nearest place I could have got the brakes fixed, but it wasn't all that far.

Driving down the A11 at 20mph, I got quite a queue of traffic behind me. I pulled off the road whenever I could, to let everything past, but I soon got another queue. Just before the place where I was going to turn off to go to Nick's village, I was stopped by the police.

"Why are you driving so slowly?" they asked. "Because my trailer brakes have failed. I'm on my way to the garage to get it fixed, I've arranged it with them."

The trailer looked very home-made, and the Land Rover and its six occupants were pretty scruffy – all legal though, as far as I knew, apart from the failed brakes. The police went over the whole outfit with a fine-tooth comb, and searched me and all my passengers for drugs, but found nothing. There was nothing to find. But they cautioned me, and took a statement about the failed brakes.

I drove on to Nick's garage, where it was decided the brakes would be too hard to fix in time for us to catch the ferry from Fishguard. Nick rang round a few other local garages, and found a car trailer we could borrow. We took the car to Fishguard and loaded it onto the ferry. Brendan's father in Cork organized for someone to take it off again at Rosslare.

We had to go back via Nick's village, to return the borrowed trailer and pick up mine. Nick hadn't repaired it by then, but without a car on it, it weighed less than the limit for an unbraked trailer.

The police actually took me to court for towing a trailer with defective brakes. I pleaded guilty by letter, but sent a letter from Nick informing the court that I had indeed arranged with him to get it fixed, and that he considered it safe as long as I drove slowly, and asked that this be taken into consideration. It was: the magistrate clearly thought the case should never have been brought. I was fined ten pounds, a nominal sum, and didn't get any points on my licence, with costs in my favour. I didn't have any costs in fact, since I'd pleaded guilty by letter, but I didn't have to pay the police costs.

SEPTEMBER 1973

I never met Roland Robertson, but it was because of him that I got my first lecturing contract. I'd just finished my PhD, and hadn't yet got my first research contract. I was at a loose end, and looked in the local paper to see what jobs were about.

Six week temporary lectureship in Motor Vehicle Engineering, at the local technical college, caught my eye. My first degree was in Mathematics, but I'd done a couple of modules in Mechanical Engineering, one of them in workshop practice; for a while between school and university I'd worked as a fitter in the bus depot where my Dad was a driver (that's another story in itself); my PhD was in engineering applications of mathematics; and I'd done all the repairs and maintenance on my own cars and some for other friends and family. I thought it was worth a shot.

It turned out that Robertson had gone to Egypt for six weeks, working at a technical college there. He was helping them to set up a course similar to the one he was running in England.

I got the job, teaching apprentice garage mechanics a bit about engineering theory. Each day of the week I had a different batch of a dozen apprentices on day release, so I got to deliver the same material five times in a week, and then something different the next week.

I was working to a predesigned course, with good course material provided by Robertson, and the apprentices had course books with sections for them to fill in, as well as excellent text and diagrams. I had some demonstrations to do, but most of my time was spent wandering around keeping an eye on the apprentices working through their books, and explaining things to them as and when they ran into difficulties.

For three of the six weeks, the afternoons were spent in the workshop, dismantling and re-assembling various sections of old cars. Three afternoons wasn't enough to cover all the sections they had to know about, but most of them had worked on some of the required sections at their garages, so it was a matter of covering the others. Not too difficult to organize. The really important thing wasn't so much them learning about the engineering anyway. It was observing the way they worked, and making sure they learnt to avoid unsafe methods of working, or unsafe behaviour.

It was quite fun. Most of the groups were good lads. I was a little worried that they might take a while to get used to the idea of an engineering lecturer who was female and half their size. I started the first session by lifting a heavy, dirty differential onto my desk and getting them to crowd round while I showed them how it worked, and that seemed to have the desired effect.

The Friday group had a couple of troublemakers in it, and regretfully I had to report them to the authorities for horseplay in the workshop, which lost them their jobs. I'd tried to warn them...

Robertson went to Egypt for six weeks again the following year. The college wrote to me and asked if I was available, which I was. They didn't even bother to advertise, so I presume they thought I'd done a reasonable job!

The best potato crop I ever had was from some I bought to eat, that decided to sprout.

The landlord, Mr Oldfield, had for many years leased the back garden of the old vicarage where I had a flat to the local council, to use as a nursery for shrubs for the parks and gardens in town, and for flowers for council functions and suchlike. Then they started to use it as a depot for machinery – mini-tractors and mowers and things – and he fell out with them, and got the lease annulled. He asked us four tenants if we wanted to take over the garden, and we did. I just shoved the old tatties in the ground.

The garden had been a nursery for so long, and had manure and compost as much as it wanted, so the soil was wonderful. One of my potatoes weighed just over 1.5 kg. *One* potato.

I also got a decent crop of (green) chick peas, at six hundred feet above sea level, in Yorkshire. The garden had seven foot high walls on three sides though, which also helped a lot I'm sure.

In 1969 Bill, Ben, Julie, Anne and I visited Norway. We went in Julie's car, and stayed in youth hostels. We had a great time.

In 1974 I went again, with Paul. We hitch-hiked and camped – until we stupidly left the tent poles behind. We didn't go back for them because we'd done a hundred miles before we realized we'd left them, and we'd waited hours and hours for a lift at that spot. After that we stayed in youth hostels. We had a great time, anyway.

One of the highlights of that trip was a lift on a cargo ship. We went down to the quay in Ålesund and asked where the ship was going, and if there was anything we could help with in exchange for a lift. The captain laughed and said the most help we could give would be to keep out of the way while the crew worked. Then he said no ship would ever give lifts like that, but that he was feeling generous, and we could keep out of way on the boat deck and he'd take us to Trondheim.

It was a lovely sunny day as we set off. We'd been up on the boat deck enjoying the view for a couple of hours, when one of the crew, smiling broadly, called us down into the crew's dining room, where they insisted we should eat with the crew. A big lamb and vegetable stew, absolutely delicious – and generous servings. Then we were shooed out of the way back onto the boat deck.

Around dusk we were called back down and fed again – grilled fish, potatoes and vegetables. After the meal, the captain said we should come onto the bridge and watch the approach to Trondheim. It was a beautiful night by then, the sky black but bright with stars, the sea black but bright with dancing reflections of the stars, and the coast each side of us black as we glided down Trondheimsfjord. Here and there we could see the lights of houses on the coast, and the occasional village; and on the water we could see the lights of the occasional smaller vessel.

Then Trondheim itself appeared round a headland – a blaze of lights. A magical evening.

It turned out that the captain was actually a Trondheim pilot, having a busman's holiday filling in for the regular captain of the vessel who was on his annual leave. He told us that we really had been very lucky, and that we didn't really have much chance of getting any more free lifts on ships.

I'd heard about Hurtigruten on my first visit to Norway. It's a ferry service that plies up and down the Norwegian coast, all the way from Bergen to Kirkenes, calling at many towns, large and small, all the way. I'd had a good look at the map and knew that Hurtigruten spends most of its time close enough to the coast to get stunning views, often in quite narrow sounds between the mainland and large islands, or even with islands both sides.

I've been dreaming of a Hurtigruten trip ever since. Well, now I've retired, and this year I've finally realized my dream. It was a wonderful holiday. I went with Ben and his wife Jean. We flew to Tromsø, then boarded the Finnmarken, in which we sailed (well, dieseled really) from Tromsø to Kirkenes, then back past Tromsø to Bergen.

I'd have liked to have seen Ålesund again – it's a particularly interesting place – but we stopped there during the night, and I didn't even wake up. We spent an afternoon, a night and a morning in Bergen, then flew back to Glasgow.

I took thousands of photographs. Now I've got a digital camera I can do that. But I don't go on holiday to take photographs – I take photographs to remember the holiday.

Hurtigruten isn't like any ordinary ferry service. From its inception in 1893 it was envisaged not only as a service carrying people, mail, and goods from one local town to another, but also as a tourist attraction. From the start, wealthy tourists had cabins, and were served good food in the dining room.

Hurtigruten ships have always been part ferry, part cruise liner in fact. The balance between the two has shifted over the years – quite noticeably in the four decades I've been conscious of Hurtigruten's existence, I think (although obviously my knowledge of the service was much less until I actually travelled on it). Talking to Norwegians in small towns, it seems that there is some concern that Hurtigruten will become even more cruise liner and less ferry in the near future, possibly giving up calling at the smaller ports altogether.

Before this holiday, I was definitely thinking in terms of being on a coastal ferry that took me on a fantastic trip, rather than being on a cruise liner. But the fact is, I've been on a cruise on a cruise liner. It was a fantastic trip, the trip of a lifetime, and there were elements of the coastal ferry about it – but far more of the cruise.

Simply viewed as a hotel, it was far and away the most sumptuous hotel I've ever stayed in, and thought of in those terms it was very reasonably priced – with the trip of a lifetime thrown in. But I'm not really a sumptuous hotel kind of person. It was certainly very comfortable, and we were certainly very well fed. But normally I'm happy to be comfortable enough and well enough fed, and to save my money for something else. If they can make a profit treating folk like that at that price, couldn't they make even more profit treating twice the number of people half as well for 60% of the price? But they've probably got their business model pretty well worked out – they've been running the service for 115 years.

We were in almost the cheapest cabins, very much the most numerous sort. There are a few a little cheaper – inside cabins without windows or portholes. And there are various more expensive cabins and suites. If you're only travelling a short distance, you can travel without a cabin, but you can't get a ticket for a long trip without a cabin. There weren't many short hop passengers. Most of the passengers were on a cruise.

There weren't many local passengers, but we delivered a lot of goods at many of the ports, fork lift trucks scurrying in and out of the cargo deck with pallets of stuff for the local supermarket or builders' merchant. The service is clearly still important in local goods transport. It runs daily in each direction, eleven ships each taking eleven days to do the round trip. (So you meet another Hurtigruten ship twice a day, every day, one around nine in the morning, and one around nine at night. This means, if you do the whole round trip, you see everywhere in daylight in one direction or the other – in summer, anyway.)

I thought about the issue of carbon footprint. Big ships use less fuel per tonne km than small ships, and big ships are the best transport there is in those terms. For goods transport, assuming your goods aren't perishable and the extra time taken moving them isn't an issue, that's the end of the story. Taking coal or oil or steel or manufactured goods around the world, large ships are the transport of choice. Fuel consumption per tonne km is also less if the ships go more slowly, which may be acceptable for some goods.

But it's not the same for passengers. You can cram passengers into a plane or a bus for a few hours in a way that would be quite unreasonable for days on a ship. A plane weighing 400 tonnes (at take off) might carry 420 passengers and use 140 tonnes of fuel to travel 13,000 km in 14 hours – that's 77 mpg per passenger (good compared to a car with just the driver, but poor compared to a full car – and very poor indeed compared to a full bus or train). Finnmarken, the ship we travelled in, weighs 15,000 tonnes (gross) and carries 1,000 passengers, and does about 42 mpg (equivalent) per passenger. That's taking no account of any goods carried – but I don't think that's a large part of the ship's budget, either in financial terms or in tonnage. The cargo deck has about 1/8 the volume of the passenger accommodation.

Our trip involved flying 2,000 miles and travelling 2,150 miles in Finnmarken. So all in all, our holiday of a lifetime for three had a carbon footprint comparable to half a typical annual mileage in one car.

The relative safety of different modes of travel is something that most people have misconceptions about. They're not helped by official statistics, indeed official statistics add to the confusion.

It's not that the statistics are actually inaccurate, it's that the impression they give is inaccurate. I'm inclined to believe that the statistics are accurate, but I don't know for sure whether they are or not. The impressions they give, and the beliefs many people hold as a result, are not actually supported by the statistics, even if the statistics are true.

The basic statistic involved is the 'fatalities per passenger mile' figure – which is claimed to be lower for flying than for any other major mode of travel, probably truthfully.

On the face of it, 'fatalities per passenger mile' looks like an appropriate measure of travel mode safety. If railways carry ten times as many passengers as airlines, and have five times as many fatalities, then other things being equal, they seem to be twice as safe. Other things aren't equal though. Passengers on planes on average travel much further than train passengers, so that's a factor in the plane's favour. But let's examine this more closely.

What we really want to know is whether it's safer to travel by plane or by train, on the journeys we actually want to make.

We don't have enough information here to make any kind of sensible judgement at all. Plane accidents are much more likely to occur near the beginning or (intended!) end of a flight, rather than while cruising at altitude between airports. Likewise, railway accidents are much more likely to occur at railway junctions or road intersections than on long stretches of uncomplicated track between cities. This means that the statistics of accidents per passenger mile, for both trains and planes, are strongly dependent on the length of the journeys. Shorter flights, with a larger proportion of their mileage close to the airports of departure and intended arrival, are less safe (per passenger mile) than long flights; likewise, short train journeys, with a larger proportion of their mileage in the cities of departure and intended arrival, are less safe (per passenger mile) than long train journeys.

If you're travelling thousands of miles, in general you don't have the option of travelling by train, and if you're travelling ten or twenty miles, in general you don't have the option of travelling by plane. It's only for distances of a few hundred miles where you have both options – and those are the least safe flights, and the safest train journeys. Which is actually safer? You can't tell from the simple "fatalities per passenger mile" figure. And that's the only figure they're going to give you.

You can't drive from the living room to the kitchen, either; and you can't (in general) walk twenty miles to work and back. But going a mile to school, which is safer, driving or walking? Simple statistics for accidents per passenger mile in cars versus accidents per pedestrian mile don't tell you.

One has to give officialdom the benefit of the doubt, and suppose that this confusion is due to their incompetence, but it's sometimes hard not to think the obfuscation is deliberate. Airlines are the main beneficiaries of these particular misconceptions.

You have to look at statistics carefully. The implications are often not what they at first appear to be. This may or may not be deliberate misrepresentation; sometimes whoever is presenting the statistics may themselves misunderstand the implications. Very often the information you really want is actually not possible to deduce from what is presented, as in this case.

Statistics, if properly done, can be very useful in assessing relative risks – but they're not often properly done, and even less often properly presented.

Paul and I were riding our bicycles up the Stanningley Bypass. We turned off onto the slip road to go into Stanningley. This is quite a long slip road. It's a wide single lane dividing into two lanes, left for Pudsey and right for Stanningley, with traffic lights at the end. Halfway up the slip road, I looked round to check there was nothing coming up behind us. There wasn't. I indicated right and pulled over to the right-hand side of the lane, ready to go into the right-hand lane and turn right at the lights.

Paul, a couple of dozen yards behind, didn't move over immediately. When he looked round, there *was* something coming – crazily fast. The car zoomed between us at a lunatic speed, missing me by millimetres according to Paul, who saw more clearly than I could. The driver had to slam his brakes on hard at the lights, which turned red too soon for him to consider jumping them – indeed, he'd have hit a car going the other way if he had.

We caught up with him at the lights. I was pretty wound up, having been badly scared by the close encounter. I brought my hand down *hard* on his roof. I know this makes a wonderfully loud noise inside a car!

He jumped out of the car. He was a big bloke, but he didn't threaten me physically. He said, "I'm a police officer," flashed his warrant card and told me to get in the car. "What will you do with my bicycle?" I asked. "Put it in the back of the car," he said. "There isn't room." There wasn't, which was obvious. "Your friend can look after it."

Fortunately Paul was right on the ball. "Friend? I'm just a witness." quoth he. I managed to keep a straight face. "Tell you what," Paul said, "We'll follow you to the police station, it's not far."

Amazingly, the officer accepted this solution.

It's funny how slowly one can ride a bicycle when one wants to. I doubt he got out of first gear all the way. There were a couple of places where we could have disappeared down alleyways wide enough for bikes but not for a car. He was probably beginning to wish we would. But we had other plans. We followed him all the way.

The police station is close to the roundabout where the road through Stanningley meets the end of the bypass again. You have to go three quarters of the way round the roundabout, then leave the roundabout onto the Farsley Ring Road, and finally turn right into the police station car park.

But not if you're on a bike. While he was going round to the car park, we jumped off our bikes, walked them across the road, and straight in through the front of the police station. By the time he arrived, we'd told the whole story to the station sergeant, and were in the process of lodging an official complaint.

Statements were duly taken. He said I'd dented his roof. We all duly traipsed out to the car park to inspect the dent. There really was a dent in the roof – but the paint had cracked at one edge of the dent, and there was rust along the line of the crack. It was obvious that it wasn't a new dent. He'd presumably known there was a dent there but hadn't realized it was so obviously old.

We didn't hear any of his colleagues sniggering, but we guessed they probably were.

I actually received a letter of apology from the Chief Constable himself. He didn't mention the lie about the dent, but I'm sure that was what clinched the case in the mind of the station sergeant.

The funniest thing about this is that I've only ever twice banged on the roof of cars by way of venting my anger with drivers, and on the other occasion it turned out to be a policeman, too.

Many, many years later, I was riding home from the station on my folding bicycle, a Raleigh Shopper. Just as I was coming around the corner by the Angel Pub, a car overtook me much too close. I was leaning over quite a bit, taking the corner quite fast, and he caught my right heel. I was put badly off balance, and tried to steer to correct. I'm quite good at recovering in this kind of situation, but was obviously going to hit the kerb in the attempt, so I stepped through the bike and ended up running across the pavement half carrying the bike. I was shaken but unhurt, and nothing was obviously wrong with my bike, either.

Unsurprisingly, I caught up with him again in the traffic – and banged on his roof. He got out looking dangerous, so I scarpered quick. Then, from a safe distance, I took a note of his registration. To make sure he didn't catch up with me again, I turned left up Juniper Hill, which is closed to motor vehicles.

But he followed me! However, he obviously had never been there before. It's not wide enough for a car to get past a bike, and the gate at the top isn't wide enough for a car at all. I didn't hang around to watch him reversing all the way back down.

At this point I still had no idea who he was.

I threaded my way through the alleyways in the town centre to the police station, and told them the whole story. They checked the registration I gave them against the DVLA database – and looked very surprised. "That's a British Transport Police vehicle!" But it was the right make and model and colour.

I didn't press the issue, and haven't ever heard anything more about it. I wish I had pressed the issue though. I'm pretty sure that was the event that started the crack in the frame that finally killed that bike a few weeks later. I saw the same chap, with the same car, at the station a few times over the next few weeks. He pretended not to recognize me. I wondered if someone had said something to him.

In case you've got the impression that I have a pretty poor opinion of the police, I'd better set the record straight. I do have a pretty poor opinion of some police officers, there's no doubt about that; and some police forces seem to have more than their fair share of bad eggs, or even to be run by them at times. But not all forces are like that, and neither are all individual officers. Whether they're a majority or a minority is impossible for me (or anyone else) to know. It's not the kind of thing one can collect statistics about in any meaningful way.

The support I got from the (male) police officers on duty at my local police station, the night I turned up in my nightie outside their first-floor back window, was first rate. I'm sure my brother-in-law Gareth was, before he retired, as lovely a police officer as you could hope to meet, as lovely on duty as he is in his private life.

One of Jyoti's brothers in India is a police officer, too. I've no idea whether he's a good egg or a bad 'un. Jyoti suspects he's seriously corrupt, sad to say. A Christian, and a pillar of the local church, apparently – but that makes no difference. There's good and bad wherever you look.

Here's another example where I've nothing but praise for a few police officers – the same force as the lot who couldn't find the thugs who trashed my flat, and not so many years later – dedicated police officers looking after the interests of a member of the public. A scruffy, long haired, anarchistic youth at that.

My friend Ed had an old Land Rover, very similar to mine, but long wheelbase whereas mine was a shorty. He'd seen it rotting away in a field, and asked the farmer if he could buy it. The farmer was delighted to get fifty quid for it. Ed got me to bring it home for him on my trailer, the one I'd made to take Brendan's car to Fishguard, by this time repaired.

Ed spent every spare moment for the next few weeks doing it up. He did a beautiful job.

He took all the bodywork off and welded up the chassis where necessary. He rivetted patches into the bodywork where the aluminium had rotted around the attachment points to the chassis.

He dismantled the engine down to the last nut and washer and rebuilt it with all new piston rings and bearing shells. It ran like a dream.

Following my advice, when he put the bodywork back on, he insulated the aluminium from the steel with nylon washers and sleeves to stop electrolytic corrosion of the aluminium, and used stainless steel nuts and bolts with PTFE tape (plumbers' tape) in the threads to stop crevice corrosion. This meant he had to use wired return instead of "earth" return for all the wiring, but that's a better job anyway.

He gave it a beautiful paint job, and informed the DVLA (or whatever it was called in those days, I forget) about its new colours.

I used to work on my own hydraulic brakes. I trusted my own work more than I trusted any garage. But Ed didn't trust himself to do the brakes. He got a local garage to do them for him. Big mistake. I hope the mechanics involved weren't any of my former apprentices!

Ed took several of our friends out for a day in the hills the first weekend after it was finished. I couldn't go, I had too much work to do. On the way home late that evening, they were descending a long, steep hill when the brakes failed. Ed pumped them as hard as he could, but there was nothing there at all.

He tried the handbrake. In something of a panic, he probably pulled it on too hard – whatever, the effect was disastrous. Series I Land Rovers (probably later ones as well, but I don't know the workings of them so well) have the handbrake on the back end of the gearbox, not on the wheels, so the braking force is transmitted via the transmission.

Well, a loaded Land Rover descending a steep hill quite fast puts a pretty large torque on the halfshafts if you pull the handbrake on hard. One of them sheared, leaving him with no handbrake – and no engine braking, either.

In fact, if Ed hadn't been panicking, he'd surely have realized that the handbrake, and the engine braking, would have worked on the front axle, if he'd shoved it into four wheel drive. Not a nice thing to do while moving, but possible if you get the engine revs right to match your speed, and what's a nasty bit of wear on the four wheel drive engagement dogs compared with rolling out of control down a steep hill? Whatever, he didn't do that.

He did what he could to save his life and that of his passengers. There's a right-angled bend under a railway bridge at the bottom of that particular hill. The last thing Ed wanted to do was crash into the abutment wall at speed!

All the way down the hill, there are little old houses each side of the road. Ed suspected that if he'd crashed into any of those, they'd have fallen down around him. Not good for the occupants of the houses, and not good for the occupants of the Land Rover, either.

But outside many of those houses there were cars – some big, some small. Ed deliberately crashed the Land Rover into the back of a smallish car. The Land Rover slowed, but didn't stop. The two vehicles slewed around a bit, and shortly the Land Rover left the other car behind.

Ed used several cars like that, trying to slow down. He eventually did crash into the bridge abutment, but not going terribly fast, and with the remains of a couple of other vehicles in front of him. Ed and all his passengers were able to climb out of the wreckage, battered and bruised but not seriously injured – not one of them.

They got away from the wreckage as quickly as they could, afraid it would all catch fire. It didn't.

Of course people all down the hill were brought out of their houses by the noise, and were pretty upset about what had happened to their cars. Someone rang the police – probably more than one someone. Fortunately at least some of the people realized that Ed and his friends were more in need of tea and sympathy than getting beaten up.

The police breathalysed Ed, who fortunately was – unlike some of his friends – stone cold sober. They took statements. They took the Land Rover away for examination, and local garages were called to take the other wrecks away.

Why is this a pro-police story? It's the care the police took over examining the Land Rover. They established the cause of the brake failure – a small piece of grit in a brake pipe connection, causing a slow leak of hydraulic fluid – and confirmed Ed's diagnosis of what had happened when he pulled on the handbrake. They helped Ed with a letter to his insurance company, who then sued the garage who'd done Ed's brakes.

I've always stopped if I've wanted to engage four wheel drive in a Land Rover, but doing it while moving would be no worse than changing from low to high ratio on the transfer gearbox on the move, without using the clutch, and I've done that a few times. The reason for that is another story.

From time to time, the Evansganj Mission Hospital runs eye camps in some of the remoter villages. A visiting eye specialist doctor and a local optometrist, together with the Evansganj missionary doctor and some other Evansganj mission staff pile into a couple of Land Rovers, put all the equipment they need onto a big trailer behind one of the Land Rovers, and head off into the jungle.

A little aside: jungle doesn't mean what you perhaps think it means. It's a Hindi word – जंगल or jangal – meaning simply wilderness, not necessarily tropical rainforest. That said, the jungle around Evansganj is mostly thickly forested; but except during the monsoon, pretty dry.

On one occasion, I was invited to accompany the team to an eye camp in Parapani, a village thirty miles beyond Navadih. They were particularly keen that I should take some photographs, some for publicity material to help raise money for further eye camps, and some for training material for medical students. The latter involved taking photographs of eye operations in progress – very interesting, but not easy to get good pictures.

We didn't leave Evansganj until an hour before sunset, after all the staff had had a day working in the hospital. It was dark before we got to Navadih, and the road beyond that point is really rough. Not to worry, Gopal is a really experienced driver.

The other Land Rover, with the big trailer, had left hours earlier. They didn't want to drive that combination in the dark.

Ten miles beyond Navadih, Gopal pressed the clutch to change down a gear to descend into a ravine we had to cross – and the clutch pedal went to the floor without doing anything. He pushed the lever out of gear, turned off the engine, and braked to a halt.

"What's the matter?" asked Dr Shah.

"Clutch failed. I'll top up the fluid." Gopal replied.

Gopal had hydraulic fluid in the toolbox. We got another three miles before the clutch failed again, and we ran out of clutch fluid long before we got to Parapani.

"We're stuck," Gopal said. "I'll walk to Parapani, and bring the other Land Rover back to pick everyone up and take you all to Parapani, then tow this one back to Evansganj for repair."

Well, I know Land Rovers pretty well. I'd driven a Land Rover without a clutch before – okay, a Series I with a mechanically operated clutch, not a Series II with a hydraulic one, but the gearbox is much the same, and the clutch becomes irrelevant when it's permanently engaged.

"Don't worry, Gopal, you can drive it without a clutch. I'll explain how."

But I ended up driving it myself.

With a low ratio, you can start the vehicle in gear – the starter motor doesn't have a problem turning the engine and moving the whole vehicle, in first gear of low ratio. The difficult bit is changing gear, especially getting up from low ratio to high ratio. With no clutch, you have to push it out of gear, then very carefully match the engine revs for the new gear, and then push it into gear. Tricky, but doable.

I drove it back to Evansganj the same way, after the eye camp.

It needed a new clutch master cylinder – not an easy thing to get in India. I went all the way to Bombay (as Mumbai was then called) to try to get one. We could order one from England, but it would take ages to arrive and get through all the bureaucracy.

I'd had a good look at how it all worked before leaving for Bombay. I realized that with a fairly simple adaptor plate, a brake master cylinder out of a Mahindra could do the job equally well. I'd seen an engineering workshop in Evansganj that seemed to have the equipment needed to make the adaptor plate, although what they actually called themselves was a sewing machine repair workshop. When I got back, I went down there to see if they'd do it for me.

I didn't arrive there until about six in the evening. We spent a good hour discussing the problem, drawing little diagrams on scraps of paper with a stub of pencil. I left the Land Rover's dead master cylinder and a nice new Mahindra one with them, and they said they'd see what they could do.

I was staying at Uncle John's. Chhoti left for work the following morning just after dawn. Not long afterwards a boy turned up at Uncle John's house asking for me, saying there was a parcel for me at the hospital.

It was the two master cylinders, the Mahindra one bolted onto a beautifully made adaptor plate. It fitted perfectly, and I had the vehicle back on the road in no time.

I went down to the workshop to thank them, and see how much I owed them.

"Oh, nothing Miss. We only used a tiny bit of old scrap metal."

"What about your time?"

"For the Mission Hospital? No charge."

What more can you ask? They aren't even Christians, they're Sikhs.

Their lathe looks old and worn out, but they can do wonders with it. It's a big lathe that they got ex-military surplus. It wasn't even designed for precision work, but they've made their own jigs and steadies for it that let them work to very fine tolerances.

I don't have a picture of the tiny girl who followed me for a long way in Bombay during that visit. Her motive wasn't to have her picture taken, as it always was with the children in the villages.

I felt a tug at my kameej and looked behind me. She must have been about four. She looked up at me with big round eyes and said, "Das paise?"

Das paise means ten paise – one tenth of a rupee. Even at that time that was very little, but not absolutely nothing.

I didn't want to give her das paise, because firstly I knew it would go to her big brother or someone like that, not to her, and secondly I'd end up being pestered by every beggar in Bombay. So I said, "Jao", which means "go away". She followed me, tugging at my kameej and saying, "Das paise?" – for about two miles. At that point I came across a chap selling oranges on the street – so I bought half a dozen, and gave her one. That didn't go to her minder – she ate it there and then. You should have seen her face; it will stay with me forever.

One good thing about the early Land Rovers was the ease of maintenance. I could dismantle almost any part of mine down to the last nut and washer, and rebuild it in a few hours, using a very basic tool kit. There was nothing at all I couldn't do in a couple of days, with no special tools that I couldn't either buy cheaply or make myself quite easily. You need so much specialized equipment to work on modern ones that many jobs are simply not possible for a private individual.

The Land Rovers the Evansganj hospital had were old. Not as old as my own in England, but old. You could work on them. But in India, getting spares was a nightmare.

I reckon the hospital would be better off running Indian Mahindras, but you can't tell them that. Land Rovers are British, they must be better. That attitude is far from universal in India, but it's still quite common, and certainly strong in the Evansganj Christian community, despite Uncle John's protestations.

To an extent, they're right. The Mahindras are undoubtedly not as strong or as reliable as Land Rovers, but you can get the spares. They probably break down two or three times more frequently, but when they do, the spares are cheap and readily available.

I used to love those old Land Rovers. I'm not so keen on the more recent ones. Like other Chelsea tractors, they're perfect for towing overweight caravans or fancy boats on motorways, but they're not very good off road: too heavy, and overpowered.

The latest Range Rovers don't even have the ground clearance you need for typical off-road driving.

It was fun driving my old Land Rover cross country, but I regret it now. I didn't feel guilty at the time, because I hadn't thought about the issue at all. It was seeing the damage done by off-roaders in Iceland that made me think about it.

When we were driving on those green lanes in the 70s, we were doing so with the tolerance (possibly the ignorance) of the landowners. Theoretically we probably should have had their permission, which we never did. I think they're pretty well all – very likely all – private roads, with no right of public vehicular access. (Who owns the land, when you're talking about square miles of wilderness, is another interesting question that I don't intend to go into here.)

At least I never did much damage to the tracks. I didn't dig deep ruts or break through the cover of vegetation, because I didn't suffer from

A lovely day out in the Yorkshire Dales, mid-1970s. Should we have done it? I don't really know. I wouldn't do it today. And I certainly wouldn't do it in a modern, overweight, overpowered SUV. No my friends didn't ride on the top while we were going along! Not without a roof rack... 8~)

wheelspin. Well, very rarely. That's because the vehicle was much lighter and less powerful than modern 4x4s.

You don't want lots of power for driving off road. It makes it much harder to avoid wheelspin, even with all your wheels driving. The combination of excessive weight with a tendency to suffer from wheelspin means that such vehicles dig themselves into the mud very easily, not only annoying the driver, but also damaging the track.

With skill and care, you *can* drive an overpowered 4x4 on mud and grass without wheelspin, but it's not easy. Some of them have traction control systems that purport to prevent it, but in reality all they do is stop it quickly when it starts, which is better than nothing but still nowhere near as good as skilful driving and a sensible power to weight ratio. A skilful driver can see the road ahead and anticipate – an automatic system can only react to what's already happened. And of course no amount of skilful driving can do anything about all that excess weight.

This section isn't a reminiscence, it's a short story I wrote for fun, but it's a realistic snapshot of Indian life. I've never actually spent any time near the sea in India, apart from that one visit to Mumbai (then Bombay), and I didn't see much of the see then.

Simon skipped breakfast that morning. He cleaned his teeth, swallowed a glass of water, and set off before dawn, pushing his bicycle the five miles into the village. He arrived long before Sushila's father opened the shop, but he knew that if he banged on the shutters someone would ask who it was, and he knew they wouldn't turn him away.

Sushila answered, and her big brother Premdas mended his chain for him cheerfully enough. "That's the third time in less than two weeks, Simon. You really need a new chain – and you should change the sprocket and the chain wheel too, they're terribly worn and they'll spoil your new chain if you don't."

Simon knew Premdas was right, and wasn't just trying to make a few extra rupees out of him. But how could he afford the 280 rupees? Even just a new chain would stretch his budget, but how often was he shelling out three rupees to have his chain fixed? And it always broke at the most inconvenient times, too.

He thanked Premdas, and then cycled back past his house to the little cove where he kept his canoe. He hid his bicycle behind the usual rock, and paddled out to sea for the morning's fishing.

It wasn't a good morning. By eleven o'clock – at a guess – he hadn't caught anything. For the thousandth time, he cursed the big boats further offshore that were sweeping the sea clean of fish. He remembered how, before they came, he could fill the bottom of his canoe in an hour or two.

Then he struck lucky. It was a big one. Once he got it on board, he could see just how big it was. Curled right round, it only just fit in his jhola. It must have weighed at least five or six kilo – enough to pay for a new chain, chainwheel and sprocket – very nearly. He knew Sushila's father would lend him the rest.

He set off back to the shore in high spirits. He pulled his canoe above the high water mark, and ran behind the rock to get his bicycle.

It had gone.

He was sure that someone had simply borrowed it, and that he'd get it back all right; but in the meantime, how could he get to the market in the village before his fish went off in that heat?

What use is a fish without a bicycle?

EVENTS OF FRIDAY 29TH JULY 1977, AS REMEMBERED BY PC MIKE THORNBER. REPRODUCED HERE WITH HIS PERMISSION.

02:07

"Good God! What's that noise?"

"Sounds like someone pretty desperate banging on a window to me. What's wrong with the bloody door? It's wide open!"

"Sounds like it's upstairs, to me, whatever it is. But how the hell did anyone get up there? You keep an eye on the desk, I'll pop upstairs."

Joe ran upstairs at the double, and was back down again even quicker.

"Call Central and get a WPC out here sharpish. I'm getting the ladder..." He was out the door and if he said anything else, I didn't catch it. I'd no idea what was going on, but Joe obviously had now, and if he thought we needed a WPC, we needed a WPC. I called.

"Hello Central. It's Mike at Burnfield. We need a WPC, as soon as you can get her here."

"Okay, Sheila's here. What should I tell her?"

"Nothing, I don't know what she's needed for yet – Joe told me to call you for one, but I didn't catch the rest of what he said and he's outside now."

"She's on her way, anyway."

"Thanks. I'll be in touch again as soon as I know what's going on, anyway."

The banging had stopped.

I got up, went to the door, and looked out into the street. All quiet, but I could hear the rattle of the ladder in the yard. Not a soul about; as long as I kept within sight of the door, I could take a look around, but before I'd gone more than a couple of yards, Joe appeared out of the yard gate with a little girl in her nightie in tow.

"She was on the cycle shed roof! She's a bit shook up, but I'm sure she'll tell us all about it in a minute."

"I'm not really much shook up, I was just out of breath, that's all." I noticed she was still panting a bit though.

"But if there's only two of you, you need reinforcements. He's still somewhere around. You've got to find him."

Yikes, I thought, *she's a lot older than she looks.*

"Okay," Joe said, "Come into the station and tell us all about it. There's a policewoman on the way – isn't there, Mike? – and we can call more reinforcements if we think we need them when you've told us what this is all about."

"Have you got a blanket or something? I'm freezing."

Joe took his jacket off and gave it to her. "I don't think we have," he said. I couldn't help noticing how funny she looked in Joe's jacket. She was tiny.

"Now. What's the story? How the hell did you come to be on the cycle shed roof?"

"My boyfriend's on the loose somewhere with a knife, he's completely crazy."

"And you jumped onto the cycle shed roof to get away from him? That's nine feet up!"

"No, no. I jumped out of the bedroom window onto our kitchen roof, than ran along the tops of the garden walls all the way up the street. Then I couldn't get down. At least Paul isn't nimble enough to have followed me along the wall tops, he's somewhere on the street, I think."

"Your boyfriend broke into your house?"

"No, we share the house. You think I'm just a little girl, don't you? I'm twenty-eight!"

"And you share your house with a crazy boyfriend?" I was beginning to wonder *who* exactly was crazy – well, maybe not just beginning.

"He didn't used to be crazy. He's only been crazy for a few weeks, and he's never been as crazy as this before. Well, he beat up his boss a few weeks ago, that was the beginning, but since then he's not been too bad until tonight. But aren't you going to get some reinforcements? You need to find him before he hurts someone – or himself."

"Sheila'll be here in a minute. She'll stay with you. Two big burly policemen are enough to catch your lad, aren't we?"

"He's six foot four and strong as an ox. And crazy, and he's got a knife. And you don't know exactly where he is by now, either. Two of you can't exactly comb the area without help."

She's all there, considering she's just escaped from a mad knifeman. If she really has, I thought, but I didn't say anything about that. "Okay, us two will stick together. We'll start by visiting your house – he could be still there, or near there – and we'll get reinforcements as soon as we can."

"I'll call Central right away. Not that they'll have many chaps free at this time of night." Joe was obviously less doubtful about the truth of the girl's story than I was. He called.

"Hello Central. Joe at Burnfield here. How many men can you get to us, quick as possible?"

"We could spare a couple of chaps – four if you're that desperate, but that'd only leave me on my own on the desk."

"Send two then – we'll call for the other two if we don't find our knifeman straight away."

"Okay. They're on their way."

"Thanks. We'll be in touch when we know anything more." He put the phone down.

"Now, young lady. About this knife. What's it like? How big?"

"It's our big kitchen knife. About a nine inch blade, I suppose, very sharp, pointed. I think he might have just sharpened it, too. I think that might have been the noise that woke me up. Otherwise, he was being very quiet. I didn't hear him come into the house..."

"I thought you shared the house?"

"We do, but he was away visiting friends. I was a bit worried about him, because he didn't tell me he was going, I just found a note from him when I got home from work, and he'd left his medication at home. I didn't get to sleep for ages, worrying about him. Then I heard a noise, I didn't know what it was, but I think now that he was sharpening the knife. Then I heard someone on the stairs, being very quiet – didn't know whether it was him or a burglar – then I saw him coming into the room with the knife. He stabbed the bed just where my chest would have been if I'd not rolled over and off the bed. I was out the window pretty damn quick."

Joe was right; the lass was genuine. Too much circumstantial detail for a fairy story. Joe was taking notes, but a proper statement would wait. Sheila could take it. But we ought at least to have got the lass's name. And we couldn't go looking for our knifeman until Sheila turned up.

"We ought at least to know your name – what's your name, young lady?"

"Penny Lane. Penelope Louise Joyce Lane if you want the whole lot."

Penny Lane? Really? I was beginning to wonder about her again.

She could see my reaction. "Yes, I really am Penny Lane. No I wasn't named after the Beatles song – I'm twenty-eight, remember? I was named *before* the Beatles song." Slightly, but not very, exasperated. *She's had to say exactly that a few times*, I thought, *she's genuine enough.*

Sheila arrived. Penny wanted to come with us to look for her boyfriend – Paul – but we insisted she stay with Sheila and give Sheila a statement. We got Penny's address from her and set off there first. "I don't have my key on me," she said, "He could possibly still be inside, although I'm pretty sure he came out into the back garden looking for me, then went up the side of the house into the street when he realized I was off along the tops of the walls."

We drove round to Penny's house. The back door was open, and there was no-one in the house. He must really have had murder in his mind: he'd managed to stab the knife right through the mattress, which I reckon is no mean feat. There was no doubting the young lady's story now. *Young lady? She's nearly my age. She looks about twelve.*

As we came out of the house, my radio came to life. "Mike – Geoff and Brian are at Burnfield station now. Probably best if you get yourselves up there to plan your campaign. Sheila's updated us on the situation, and is updating them now."

"Okay. We'll be there in a minute."

At the junction, I looked left before turning right towards the station, and spotted a tall young man in the middle of the road a couple of hundred yards away. "That must be him. Joe, let them know we think we've got him. Tell them to send Geoff and Brian straight here, in case he runs and we need to block escape routes."

He didn't run. He still had the knife in his hand, but he didn't offer any resistance. He just seemed very confused and dejected, and very meekly handed the knife to Joe, handle first. Geoff and Brian turned up as we were arresting him, and he sat quietly between Geoff and Joe in the back of the car as we took him back to the station.

He was admitted back into psychiatric care, and never prosecuted. Penny didn't want to press charges, and he'd not threatened anyone else or resisted arrest.

I saw Penny around a few times after that, but for several years we didn't speak to each other beyond saying hello. Then, half a lifetime later, when I'd not seen her for decades, we bumped into each other in my local pub. She'd left Burnfield long ago, and was just visiting old haunts.

We'd both retired by then, and spent a good hour chatting. She told me she was writing a book, and that the episode with Paul and the knife would be in it. We parted on the best of terms, and exchanged addresses and phone numbers. I don't suppose I'll ever see her again though – she lives in Edinburgh now.

APPENDIX I: MUSTARD OIL

I'm pretty confident that mustard oil is nutritionally the best oil there is, although this is still controversial in Europe and the USA. Its disappearance from the Indian marketplace was a disaster, and it hasn't completely regained its dominant position in the Indian market even now the ban has been lifted. It's still hard to get in some parts of India. It's less clear-cut whether this is really a scandal, although it may well be.

In Europe, Canada and the USA (possibly elsewhere, I don't know), mustard oil offered for sale must display a warning, something like NOT FOR HUMAN CONSUMPTION, or FOR EXTERNAL USE ONLY. This has been variously attributed to the likelihood of mustard oil being contaminated with *argemone seed oil*, and the fact that it naturally contains high levels of *erucic acid*.

There have been outbreaks of *epidemic dropsy* in India, where consumption of contaminated mustard oil has led to numerous deaths. The contamination has occasionally been with argemone seed oil, but more often simply with inedible industrial oils.

There have been suggestions that at least some of these outbreaks have been engineered deliberately as part of a campaign to get the previously very popular mustard oil banned, in order to make room in the Indian market for imported vegetable oils – particularly canola, but also soya bean oil, corn oil, and peanut oil. If so, it's been spectacularly successful. It's particularly the USA who have benefited – or, to be more strictly accurate, certain vested interests in the USA. US taxpayers haven't benefited at all. Without subsidies from the taxpayer the whole trade would be uneconomic, and the loss to the US taxpayers is greater than the gain to the vested interests.

Argemone is a weed which is not native to India – it originates in Mexico. Its seeds look very like the seeds of one of the main varieties of mustard grown in India, and since its introduction in India, it has occasionally been seen growing in fields of mustard. However, the plant is completely unlike the mustard plant, and is easily removed before harvesting, or even before seeds are set on either mustard or argemone. Furthermore, the normal method of harvesting mustard wouldn't harvest the argemone seeds anyway. It's almost inconceivable that accidental contamination could occur at anything more than an insignificant and harmless level. If it wasn't part of a conspiracy, then it was simply an attempt to make a bit more profit, because argemone seeds have zero value, whereas mustard seeds cost money.

A chemical test to detect argemone oil contamination in mustard oil is quite simple (on an industrial scale – not so easy at home), and sensitive to very low concentrations levels, well within safety limits.

Contamination with industrial oils can only be someone trying to make additional profit – or conspiracy, but adulteration of foodstuffs with cheaper lookalike materials is sadly not uncommon in India anyway, with occasionally disastrous results.

Probably the political coup of banning mustard oil took advantage of a chance cluster of serious contamination incidents, rather than the incidents themselves been part of a coordinated campaign – but who knows? Long experience of the total unscrupulousness of powerful vested interests is bound to make one suspicious.

Erucic acid naturally forms about 40% of mustard oil. Whether it's toxic in humans is highly doubtful – epidemiological studies have failed to show any correlation whatsoever with the health problems found in rats fed high levels of erucic acid in their food. Nonetheless, the Food Standards Agency in the UK, and other food regulation bodies around the world, have insisted that foods containing high levels of it must not be sold.

FOOD STANDARDS AUSTRALIA NEW ZEALAND published a technical report:

ERUCIC ACID IN FOOD:

A Toxicological Review and Risk Assessment

TECHNICAL REPORT SERIES NO. 21

June 2003

I hope it's still available online:

http://www.foodstandards.gov.au/_srcfiles/Erucic%20acid%20monograph.doc

It gives, in considerable detail and honestly as far as I can make out, the scientific basis of its advice. It concludes that the safe level of erucic acid in vegetable oil for human consumption is around 2%. This is high enough to pass canola as fit for human consumption, but too low to pass mustard oil.

To reach this conclusion, it first establishes that nursling piglets are, of all the animals tested, the most susceptible to erucic acid poisoning. It then takes the levels of erucic acid that are safe for nursling piglets, and divides by a hundred to establish a safe level for human consumption, allowing a safety factor.

Would that such stringent tests were applied to foodstuffs – and other things that one is liable to ingest or inhale – produced in the US or Europe! And this for a foodstuff that has been consumed for millenia...

The section of the report entitled *Effects in humans* is particularly illuminating. It goes into considerable detail about deaths of humans in areas (France, Spain and India) where the consumption of rapeseed oil (also high in erucic acid) or mustard oil is traditional. They found NO evidence that erucic acid had any adverse effects whatsoever in humans, despite finding erucic acid in the bodies from areas where it's present in the diet.

"The presence of significant amounts of erucic acid in the myocardium could not be associated with any observed heart damage." (India: over 100 cases in Calcutta where there was a lot of mustard oil in the diet, 63 cases in areas where there wasn't)

"a significant association with alcohol consumption was found, but none could be established with dietary fat and vegetable oil consumption." (France: 269 cases)

"the oil was, in fact, a mixture of industrial rapeseed oil, soybean oil, olive oil, and animal fats that had been purposely denatured with 2% aniline and was never intended to be used as an edible oil" (Spain: hundreds of deaths from consumption of "rapeseed oil", May 1981 – aniline really IS poisonous!)

That's the question of whether mustard oil is harmful or not: I'm absolutely certain that it's not. Whether there's an actual conspiracy behind the way it's been denigrated is impossible for me to tell.

Now for the question of its nutritional value.

As far as I can make out from a variety of sources, an oil for human consumption should ideally contain a high percentage of unsaturated fat, a good percentage of which should be ω-6 (omega-6) and ω-3. The ratio of ω-6 to ω-3 should be in the range 1:1 to 4:1.

Mustard oil fits this description better than any other vegetable oil, almost all of which have much higher ratios of ω-6 to ω-3, and most of which have lower percentages of unsaturated fat as well. Few other vegetable oils contain as much ω-3 as mustard oil – soya bean oil is an exception, containing about the same amount of ω-3, but a much larger amount of ω-6, skewing the ratio badly (almost 10:1).

Fish oils typically have even lower ratios of ω-6 to ω-3 than mustard oil. Sometimes the ratio is even lower than 1:1. You can balance out vegetable oils with a high ratio by consuming comparable quantities of fish oil.

Of course you can obtain fish oil simply by eating the fish. You don't have to buy supplements. If you gut the fish yourself, learn to identify the liver and heart and don't throw them away!

In Britain I cheerfully buy mustard oil labelled *Pure Mustard Oil, For External Use Only,* and cook with it. I'm not dead yet. It's exactly the same stuff hundreds of millions of Indians used for millenia before the ban, and are using again now the ban's been lifted in India – although the market still hasn't recovered completely by any means, it's still hard to get mustard oil in some parts of India, and in some areas the farmers still can't find a buyer for the mustard seed.

APPENDIX II: SIDDHARTH SURANA'S BLOG ON SLUM DWELLERS, REPRINTED WITH HIS PERMISSION.

We all must have noticed ever increasing number of people living in shanties along the roads or sleeping on footpath. In metros like Delhi and Mumbai, I've seen such pitiful (sometimes sickening) sights of slum/footpath dwellers' lives. It pains me to think how human life can be so degraded. Where from have these people come? Were all of them born thus, without a piece of roof on their heads? Why are they in this condition? For sure, not by choice, unlike what some of us like to believe. Given a choice, no human being would like to live a life of a rat in these four foot square holes covered with plastic rags; to get run over by some rich drunkard coming back from a late night party or to get washed away in floods without leaving a trace behind.

Most of these people come from places like some tribal village in Dungarpur, from the hills of Uttaranchal, or the forests of Chhattisgarh, where they have been living a respectable life, albeit within limited means. They had their land, cattle, or even small scale enterprise there. Some of them have left behind some beautiful crafts of which they were masters. As India begun to embark on the path of fast economic growth coupled with massive industrialization, their skills and abilities started to become obsolete. Further, the 'democratic' government in collusion with business houses took over their land for 'developmental' purposes at low rates of compensation without providing alternative employment or arable land. Means of livelihood dwindled down in their native places and the survival instinct brought these people to bigger cities.

Sure they use the urban infrastructure without paying for it, like filling water from some broken pipeline nearby or tiny amounts of electricity to light up a 100 watt bulb. But do we ever realize how much they contribute to the urban economy in form of cheap labor? Faces of the kaamwali, sabziwala, dhobi and the ubiquitous chhotu in the neighborhood restaurant promptly come to mind. From construction laborers to rag-pickers, they all contribute in their own way while living on the edge. They produce more than they consume. Do we ever stop to think, had these people not been living on so little or had they been paying for house rent, water and electricity, how much would their services cost us? In a way, they are subsidizing our cost of living and in the process trying to achieving their sole objective of survival.

Such is the hypocrisy of our society that we all want to benefit from the cheap services/products but when it comes to taking moral high ground we don't think twice before branding them as illegal inhabitants. Since their lives are not formally 'registered', the society is free to disown them or even deny their existence at its convenience.

Jhaggis (like slums only much worse) in Mumbai. Some of the people living in these little homes made out of other people's rubbish survive by sifting through the rubbish in the foreground, finding any recyclable materials they can sell; others are working building the blocks of flats in the background. They'll never be able to afford to live anywhere like that, though.

This was December 1983, but you can still see sights like this all over India.

GLOSSARY

Adivasi – the indigenous tribal people of India. Literally, aboriginal – and proud to be so. Mostly living in remote rural areas, but increasingly also present in the cities, mostly but not all in poverty. Outside the caste system altogether, but often very badly treated by rich or high caste Hindus.

Ayah – mother. Well that's what it means to an ordinary Indian, but so far as British children growing up in India during the British Raj were concerned, their mother was Mother, and the Indian lady who looked after them was their Ayah. (Ayah is also the past tense of *to come*, but that's just an example of a homonym.)

Chhoti – small or little, or little one (feminine). A common nickname for small girls, less common for a woman.

Chhotu – a common nickname for small boys. Related to Chhota, small, or little one (masculine).

Dalit – lower caste, formerly translated into English as untouchable, and often treated like that by high caste Indians. Also called Harijan (God's People), a term coined by Mahatma Gandhi in an attempt to counter widespread prejudice against them.

Dhobi – laundryman.

Jhaggi – a tiny dwelling constructed mainly out of materials scavenged from other people's rubbish. A jhaggi dweller can only dream of the luxury of living in a proper slum.

Kaamwali – a female worker, often meaning a domestic servant.

Mala – a necklace of flowers, essentially a daisy chain but with bigger, showier flowers.

Naxalite – armed revolutionary, a follower of Naxalism. Named after Naxalbari, the village in West Bengal where the movement began. Generally opposed to the oppression of the rural poor by the Indian élite, but much more complicated than that in practice.

Puja – a Hindu religious ritual, a bit like a Catholic lighting a candle and saying a little prayer.

Puri – a bit like a chapatti, but usually smaller in diameter and thicker, and made with vegetable oil (or ghee, if you're wealthy) rather than just water.

Sabji – vegetables, either curried or uncooked. In other parts of India, this might be called Sabzi.

Sabziwala (or sabjiwallah) – provider of vegetable curry.

Salwar kameej – sometimes called a Panjabi suit. Salwar is a pair of loose fitting ladies' trousers, and kameej (kameez in some parts of India) is a shift worn over them. I've heard it said that kameej is the same word as the French word *chemise,* both from Latin *camisia.*

Sarpanch – elected village headman, roughly speaking.

Shudh Hindi – 'pure' Hindi. The Hindi equivalent of the Queen's English.

Penny isn't a real person?

No, she isn't. I made her up.

She started 'life' simply as a pseudonym on the Guardian User talkboard (GUT) – an internet forum run by the Guardian Newspaper, nominally to discuss the news, politics, and current affairs both British and international, but in practice hosting all kinds of discussion and even just friendly or not so friendly chatter.

When I first posted on GUT, I used my real name, but rapidly realized that this really wasn't a good idea. But I was very afraid that people would spot me by my style and my choice of subject matter, whatever username I adopted. So I decided to create a character different enough from me that people *wouldn't* recognize me.

Apparently it worked.

I originally wanted to use *pennylane* as my username, but although no-one seemed to have been posting under that name, it was taken. I quickly thought up some initials for her. Just plain *plane* seemed silly, and *pljlane* popped into my head, so that's what she became. Female, to be obviously not me. Just to make sure everyone knew she was female, and indeed that she was Penny Lane, she signed off her posts *Penny*, as if they were letters, a thing almost no-one else was doing.

Another of her idiosyncrasies was the use of a trademark emoticon (or smiley). This emoticon was intended to represent her spectacles, her famously wonky nose, and of course the same grin everyone else uses. 8~)

She shot her mouth off on many subjects, and told lots of stories. She's not as shy as me. Oh, the freedom! She really did take on a life of her own, I couldn't help it. But she was never a *troll*. She never pretended to hold objectionable opinions, simply to wind people up. The opinions she expressed were always mine.

She made a few enemies, but she made a lot of friends, too.

Many of her posts are still there on GUT.

Eventually I (as my GU alter ego, coshipi) confessed to having made her up. The reaction was most interesting.

Some folks were scandalized – some still are. They're hiding behind pseudonyms themselves, and who knows whether their stories are true or not?

Other folks forgave me, and some didn't think there was anything to forgive. I'm friends in real life with several of each of those sorts now.

Many of the stories in this book first appeared – mostly in less detail than here – as posts on GUT. Many of them are true stories from my own past, with names changed. Many have other changes, too, to fit them into Penny's life story rather than my own, or to anonymize them. Others are entirely fictional. I'm not going to tell you which are which. You can guess to your heart's content.

One name I haven't changed is Siddharth Surana's. He's real, and he's really a friend of mine. His blog is at:

http://siddharth-surana.blogspot.com/

Take a look – I promise you it's worth it.

About the author:

Clive K. Semmens was born in London in 1949, and grew up in Yorkshire and Hertfordshire, United Kingdom. His wife hails from the place called Bartola in this book. They have two grown up children.

Clive is a multi-talented man with vast knowledge and experience of India and above all, he is a humble person. He knows French, German and Hindi well enough to be useful, but in his own words "would certainly not describe himself as fluent or accurate in any of them."

He describes his hobbies as innovative DIY (anything from microelectronics to major building projects), travel, photography, reading and writing.

He's particularly interested in people and their lives, trying to see things from the point of view of people from very different backgrounds, to avoid as far as possible making errors of judgement arising out of the unconscious assumptions of his own background.

Clive is also very interested in the world around people and is well versed in the issues surrounding energy production and consumption, resource consumption, and environmental pollution.

In 1967, he gained a scholarship from the United Kingdom Atomic Energy Authority to study Nuclear Engineering, a course intended to lead to a career designing nuclear power stations and associated infrastructure. His studies and experiences in the nuclear industry led him to the conclusion that nuclear power generation is a very bad idea, and he changed course.

After that, Clive's had a wide-ranging professional career with a long list of technology based roles as an engineer, lecturer, journals manager etc.

He first visited India in 1983, and rapidly got involved providing technical advice for a charity. He spent six months in India on that occasion, and again a year later. Since then, he and his wife have visited her relatives in India about once every couple of years.

Today they live in a small English city, retired from commercial life. They still travel, and he takes part in political and cultural discussions and writes essays and novels.

www.ingramcontent.com/pod-product-compliance
Ingram Content Group UK Ltd.
Pitfield, Milton Keynes, MK11 3LW, UK
UKHW041437180426
11947UKWH00007B/485